ENDRE

THE ELSKER SAGA

S.T. Bende

The Elsker Saga
Endre

Edited by: Lauren McKellar and Eden Plantz
Interior Snowflakes by: Eden Plantz
Cover Art by: Alerim
ISBN: 150021650X
ISBN-13: 9781500216504

First publication: 2013, S.T. Bende

DEDICATION

To my handsome princes:
Anything is possible, so long as you believe.
And to MorMorMa. For everything.

CONTENTS

CHAPTER ONE

***"OH, KRISTIA," THE HORRIBLE** keening voice sneered from the blackness in my head. I stood in a field of ice, surrounded on all sides by tall, dark mountains. The air was a damp-cold that chilled to the bone, and icicles rose from the ground like distorted turrets. The voice was familiar, but my surroundings were completely foreign.*

"Where am I, Elf Man?"

"Exactly where I want you to be," the voice hissed.

"And where is that?"

"Poised to fail. You don't really think he's going to marry you, do you?"

"You know entirely too much about my personal life. And hey, didn't I kill you already? How'd you survive?"

"Sweet Kristia." His lanky figure emerged from between the ice formations with his hands open in welcome. "It has been too long."

"Not long enough," I muttered. "And seriously, I killed you, remember? With this." I held up my necklace, the silver carving of Thor's hammer, Mjölnir, which had

belonged to my grandmother. “Don’t make me use it again.” I wielded the hammer like a shield but Elf Man just cackled.

“Please.” He waved a hand. “You wouldn’t dare. Because without me, you won’t know how to save her.”

“Save who?” I turned as Elfie made a slow circle around me. I’d never felt more like a caged animal. “Tell me, you creep. Who?”

“Ah-ah-ah.” The demon wagged his finger. “Wouldn’t want to spoil the surprise.”

“Fine. What’s going to happen to her, *whoever she is?”*

“Oh, it will be exquisite.” The man’s glee was sickening. If Webster’s dictionary published photos alongside the definitions, his image would be right next to lunatic.

“You are seriously messed up, you know that?” I pivoted, matching the elf’s pace.

“You have no idea.” He chuckled darkly. “But you will when you lose someone you love.”

“Not Ull.” I squeezed my necklace, and it warmed at my touch.

“No, not Ull. I want him to suffer every bit as much as you.”

“Sif?” I could feel my necklace start to pulse.

“I’m not telling you, poppet.” He spat out the last word. “But I will give you a hint.”

Elfie swirled his hand and mist appeared between us. It acted as a screen, showing a cavernous room I’d never seen. Bars covered the small window of a chipped wooden door. It was some kind of a jail cell. Sparks of light shot from under the door, and I heard a woman shriek. She was in pain—not any pain I'd ever known, but a pain born of torture. She screamed again, her voice frail and hoarse.

"Stop it! What are you doing to her?" I doubled over and shoved my hands against my ears to drown out the sound.

"Oh my pet, this is only the beginning. I will give her an illness that kills her body from the inside. It will eat away her spirit, eroding all goodness within her. When she is nothing but darkness, I will take her body. By then, she will welcome death."

I looked up from my crouch, squinting through the fog-screen. Elf Man was nowhere to be seen. I jumped to my feet, turning in a slow circle while my eyes scanned the frozen field behind me for a weapon. Unless I was going to kill the creep with an icicle, it looked like I was short-handed. I grabbed a crude weapon anyway, clutching my necklace in the other hand. It had started to glow.

"Come out, coward. I'm going to have to do a better job of killing you this time."

A ghostly cackle echoed off the mountain ridge, first behind me and then to my right. "But don't you see, sweet Kristia? You can never be done with me. I will follow you to the ends of this world. And the next. Until I own your soul." The voice sounded from my left, and I turned abruptly. The deranged creature stood beside me, freakishly long fingers reaching my way. His eyes caressed the contour of my neck, leaving goose bumps in their wake. As his hands twitched in time with my pulse, I narrowed my eyes.

I was not in the mood to be strangled today.

"Oh no you don't." I thrust the icicle upwards toward his abdomen, but he chopped it in half with one wiry forearm.

"Is that the best you can do?" His cold hands wrapped around my neck, cutting off the circulation. I waved the broken stump of icicle at his chest, but his arms kept me just out of reach. He lifted me slowly by the neck, my lungs screaming for air as he squeezed. I felt my eyes bulge; whether from shock or pain I wasn't sure. I wrapped my hands around Elfie's fingers and tugged. His grip loosened just enough that I could draw one ragged breath.

"How do I save her?" I croaked. Assuming I survived the next few minutes, a lot was riding on the demon's answer.

"You'd have to destroy me," Elf Man roared. "Like you ever could." He raised me over his head with one hand, shaking me violently. My head wrenched from side to side.

"Watch. Me," I panted, using all my strength to grip the silver hammer that rested at my collarbone. I squeezed as tightly as I could, a pathetic grasp, but it would have to be enough. Heat radiated from my hand as the hammer burst to life, beams of light shooting from between my fingers.

"No!" The elf released his painful grip, and I dropped to the ground. My leg exploded with pain. I opened my eyes to glare at the sharp rock that interrupted my fall.

"No!" Elfie shrieked again. I clutched my bleeding calf as I watched the light from my necklace wrap around him, chaining him with its brilliance. The coils circled his legs and wrists like manacles until he was bound to the icy field. "This is not over, poppet," he hissed before the light sealed his mouth. His muffled laughter echoed throughout the valley as I was shaken out of the horrible scene.

❄ ❄ ❄ ❄

"No." I kicked at the air, earning a sharp pain in my shin. I opened my eyes and realized I'd kicked the dashboard. Wait, dashboard? But I'd just been in a frozen hell. At least, it felt like hell—barren, dark, void of any feeling except desolation. Covered in ice. An icy hell?

"Kristia, darling." I felt Ull's cool hand on my forehead as he swiftly steered the Range Rover to the closest exit. "Darling, wake up. You are having a bad dream."

It was a dream?

"Are you having another wedding nightmare? I will rein Inga back in. I know she has been a bit . . . over-involved in the planning."

"Wedding nightmare . . ." I rubbed at my leg, trying to remember why I was in my fiancé's fancy SUV. That's right, we were headed to his English country house, Ýdalir, so his immortal grandmother could train me to become a goddess of Asgard. Just your typical weekend away from studies at Cardiff University.

Why did my subconscious have to go and ruin

everything?

"Kristia." Ull's tone dropped, sending a new kind of chill down my spine. "Please tell me you were having a wedding nightmare."

I sighed. As much as I wanted to let Ull believe I was a stressed-out bride, I knew better than to lie to him. In less than three months, Ull would allow me to give up my human life and join him in an eternal existence. The only thing he asked in return was that I give him complete access to the disturbed inner-workings of my mind.

"I had a vision," I admitted.

"You saw *him* again." It wasn't a question. Ull's brow furrowed, and he cut across two lanes of traffic to pull into a half-empty parking lot. "Tell me."

"It was awful." I recalled the worst of my dream, narrating to Ull as I went. His hands gripped the steering wheel so hard, his knuckles turned white.

"Is that all?" he asked when I'd finished.

"Yes," I whispered.

"Do you have any idea who the woman was?"

I didn't want to answer. There was only one person it could be, and Ull wouldn't be happy when I told him.

"Kristia. Do you know who the woman was?"

"Not exactly. I didn't see her face, and I don't know for sure."

"But you suspect?"

I closed my eyes. "Ull, he plans to destroy someone you love from the inside. And torture her. He couldn't do that to a god—you guys are too powerful. It has to be a human. And there's only one human who means enough to you for him to plan something this elaborate."

"You." Ull's voice cracked. "He wants to hurt you." He exhaled slowly. "He wants to take you away from me."

"I think so," I whispered. "But he's had plenty of chances. He could come and get me any time, in any dream. If he's so intent on killing me, why hasn't he done it already?"

"Who is this monster?" Ull frowned. "How is he getting into your head?"

"I have no idea. He looks like an elf—he has pointy ears, but he's tall and kind of handsome in a twisted way. Elves are ugly, right?"

"Dark elves are." Ull smoothed his features and reached out to hold my hand. "Please try not to worry, my love. So long as you are with me, I will not let anything happen to you."

"You can't save me from my dreams, Ull."

"I know." He leaned against the headrest and closed his eyes. "You do not have any idea who he is?"

"No. He's got brown hair. He's tall and skinny. Pointy ears. He never says his name."

"That could be anyone."

"I know."

"Do you have any idea where you were this time?" Ull rubbed at his forehead.

"I'd never seen anything like it. It was cold. Dark. I was in an isolated valley—big, black mountains and a field of ice."

Ull's eyes flew open. "You were in Jotunheim?"

"I don't know. Is that what it looks like?"

"Did you feel empty? Hollow?"

"Yes," I whispered.

"Unbelievably lonely?"

"Yes."

"Jotunheim." Ull clenched his jaw. "Evil."

"Frost giants, right?" I tried to remember what little Ull had told me about this other realm. Most of what I knew came from Professor Carnicke's mythology class.

"Yes. Dark elves are granted entry, too. And other . . . hostile elements are admitted. I spent a lot of time there when I was an assass—when I was working as a warrior."

That made sense. Ull had spent the majority of his existence as a warrior of Asgard, eliminating threats to the realm. If Jotunheim was as bad as he'd said, he'd probably racked up a whole heap of kills there. He wasn't proud he'd taken so many lives, so Odin had granted his request for a career change. Now, Ull protected all the realms as God of Winter.

"So this elf creep is evil. We knew that. We still don't know who he is."

"But we know who he is not. He is not a light elf; he is obviously not a Norn. He is not an Asgardian—not that I really thought one of us would be capable of hurting you. Except . . ." Ull drummed his fingers on his lap.

"Except?"

"Well, Loki has done some pretty terrible things

in his time."

"Loki? Odin's half-brother?"

"Blood brother. He kidnapped Idunn, which nearly killed us all. He chopped off my mother's hair as a joke—had to bribe the dwarves to develop gold hair to replace it, and nearly got himself killed in the process. It would not be the first time he did something to hurt the realm. But I do not believe even he could do something this terrible. He is inherently selfish; he always gets something out of his treachery. And he stands to gain nothing by hurting you. Or me."

"Besides, he isn't an elf, is he?"

"No."

"Well, this guy has pointy ears."

A look of horror crossed Ull's perfect features. "Wait! Did he have any idea what you are going to do?"

"You mean marry you, become a goddess, and spy on Asgard's enemies?"

"Does he know that you are *the Seer*?" Ull whispered the last words with reverence, and I sighed. I understood it was a big deal to be some all-knowing visionary that was prophesied way back at the beginning of time. I did. But Ull was as worrisome as he was bossy, and this whole *Seer* thing was starting to occupy a disproportionate amount of his stress-about-Kristia time.

And honestly. I was still just me.

"He knew you and I were engaged. But I don't think he knew about the other stuff."

"I do not like this. How did he know about us?"

"He's known about us from the beginning. The first

time I saw him he was freaking out about what I was going to do to his *plan*, and after that, he was all fixated on whether you were going to stay with me. It's like he's obsessed with you."

"I wish I knew what all of this means. I do not like feeling like I have no control." He shook his head. "The only thing I know I can do is take you to Olaug."

Even though our impending visit had a purpose, I didn't need a reason visit Ull's grandma. I loved spending time with her.

"We have to get you up to speed so you can help me figure out what we are dealing with. I have to know you are safe—that Ragnarok is over and this monster, whoever he is, is locked away. If he thinks he can mess with my bride, he has another thing coming." Ull emitted fury and I waited for the wave to pass. His anger should have been terrifying, but the way this trained killer fretted over me was downright adorable.

After a minute, he wiped his palms on his jeans. "We will figure it out, darling. Maybe Olaug's instruction will trigger something for you. If you recognize anyone when she talks you through the realms, please tell me."

"I will, Ull." I leaned over to kiss his cheek. "I tell you everything."

"You had better," Ull growled. "You gave your word."

"Small price to pay for an eternity with you." I kissed him again and his face softened.

"Please do not worry about this creature, Kristia. I will take care of you."

"I could say the same to you." I squeezed his hand while he pulled out of the parking lot and back onto the highway. But how could I protect us from Elf Man when I didn't even know who he was?

CHAPTER TWO

ULL DROVE THE REST of the way to Ýdalir like a man possessed. The English countryside passed in a blur outside the window of the Range Rover. Twice, I pointed out passing speed limit signs, but he ignored me.

"I'm not going to be able to help anyone if you don't get us to Olaug in one piece. It's not like ten more minutes are going to kill us."

"You are awfully bossy today."

"Said the pot to the kettle." I bit back my laughter, and even Ull had to hide a smile.

"Fine." Ull slowed to a slightly less alarming speed, and in no time we passed the sign welcoming us to Bibury. We pulled up the long drive to Ull's country house. The cathedral of trees ushered us toward the central fountain, where a collection of fish splashed happily. Ull parked, then came around to help me out of the car. It was a relief to stretch our legs after the tense drive.

Ýdalir stood in front of us, the picture of country calm. Nobody would suspect it was home base for Ull, Inga, Gunnar, and Olaug; the Norse deities who opted to masquerade as three college students—and one granny—rather than living in Asgard. The white puffs coming from the stone chimney let me know Olaug was inside waiting for us.

Ull reached out to steady me when I caught my toe on one of the stones in the driveway. It was par for the course—I was hardly the most graceful snowflake in the blizzard.

As we walked toward the cottage, Ull squeezed my hand. I smiled at his long fingers resting against my engagement ring. Its round stones were bound together in a delicate pattern that made it look like lace; sparkly, pristine, exquisite lace.

"I will take care of you, Kristia," Ull pledged. I tore my eyes off my ring to stare at him. His free hand rested in the back pocket of gently worn blue jeans, and his impressive torso was hidden beneath a grey cashmere sweater. I reached up to stroke the blond stubble that peppered his square jaw, and I couldn't help but smile at the intensity of his stare. Everything was so serious with Ull.

"You always have." I stood on tiptoe to kiss his cheek, but he wrapped one muscular forearm around my waist and pulled me into his chest. I felt his firm abdomen against mine one as Ull lowered his head to rub his nose along my jaw.

I shivered at the sensation of cool breath tickling my neck. "I've missed this."

"Me too." Ull trailed his nose to my ear. "And this," he whispered as he nipped at my earlobe. "And this." He ran his lips along my neck, planting soft kisses on my collarbone.

My eyes rolled back in my head. I grabbed Ull's shirt and pulled him close.

"Don't ever go to Asgard for a whole week again, okay?"

"Okay." Ull moved his lips up my neck to my chin before settling squarely on my mouth. My hands rose to his hair, and I wrapped my fingers in the tousled, blond strands, holding his face to mine.

"Kristia," he groaned, pushing me back just when things started to get good.

"That's what you get when you leave me on my own for seven days."

"Then I had better go away more often."

"Mmm."

Ull brought his mouth down again. He pulled me up with one arm, crushing his lips against mine and spiking my pulse to an unhealthy level. A warm glow settled in the pit of my stomach. Ull gently swept my mouth with his tongue, and the glow erupted into a ball of fire. My hands flew to his shoulders and I pulled him even closer, feeling his heart beat against my chest. Ull's free hand ran softly down my side, coming to rest just below my hip. He gave a little squeeze and sucked on my bottom lip. My breath shallowed to ragged gasps.

No wonder I didn't hear the creak of the door.

"Ull! Kristia!"

I jumped at the sound of Olaug's laughter. Ull cleared his throat as he stepped in front of me, giving me a minute to catch my breath. I tugged on my top while I consciously exhaled. As much as I adored Ull's almost-grandmother, her timing couldn't have been worse. But when Ull bent down to hug her, I couldn't help but smile at the ease between them. There weren't many people, immortal or otherwise, that Ull could be himself with. Olaug knew him better than anyone—she'd pretty much raised him.

"Hi Olaug." I gave an awkward wave. With my shirt tucked in and my hair back in place, I could administer a proper greeting. With Olaug here, we'd be able to start my training tonight. Heaven knew I had plenty to catch up on, especially now that Elfie was after me again.

"And look who is with me." Olaug stepped aside to reveal the gently wrinkled face of the immortal prophet responsible for bringing Ull and me together: my favorite Norn.

"Elsker!" I threw my arms around the tiny woman. "What are you doing here? I thought you'd be back in Asgard."

"I *was* in Asgard. Spent a few weeks catching up with everyone. But funny thing, after all these years, I got used to this realm."

"Got used to it? There's a glowing endorsement," I teased.

"You know what I mean, silly girl." She swatted at me. "I like it here."

"I'm glad." I laughed. "Does this mean you're

staying?"

"I bought the old Gardner cottage across the Coln." Elsker beamed. "Odin's reassigned me to mortal babies in this quadrant, so it makes sense to keep a base here."

"Does this mean we will see you often?" Ull hugged Elsker gently. His disheveled, blond hair flopped adorably over one eye. Even bent over, his six-foot-five-inch frame positively dwarfed the teensy Norn.

"I hope so. I spent enough time wishing you two would get together."

Olaug shook her head. "I'm the grandmother. I guarantee I wanted this more than you did."

"Well." Elsker waved her hand. "Who's measuring?"

"You were, you troublemaker."

"Don't sass me, old woman." Elsker wagged her finger and Olaug laughed.

"It doesn't take a great seer to know you two are going to get into all kinds of messes." I shook my head.

Ull led me to the table, where Olaug's famous roast was waiting. "Well, come on, ladies." He pulled out my chair. "Tell me what I missed while I was away."

While Olaug and Elsker filled Ull in on the happenings in Bibury, I took in our peculiar little gathering. The God of Winter, his handler/grandmother, the Norn who identified my very odd talent, and mortal—at least, for now—me. We certainly made an unconventional dinner party.

We ate heartily, and after a generous helping of apple pie, Elsker said her goodbyes.

"Come back tomorrow for board games?" I winked when Ull shot me a look. Board games were the one thing he was awful at.

Elsker chuckled. "Much as I would love to, I'm afraid I have to pass. Work waits for no Norn."

"Will we see you soon?" Ull asked Elsker.

"Probably not right away. I've got a fair number of projects. Springtime is big for babies in this realm." She waggled her eyebrows and pointed at me from behind her hand.

"Elsker!" Did she know something I didn't? She was a prophet, after all.

"So I won't see you for a while." She continued like it was nothing. "But I'll be at the wedding. Wouldn't miss it. And I'll help with your vision training once you're a full goddess. Thor figured it was best if I was the Norn to get that job."

"Yay." I clapped my hands.

"And don't forget you can call me through your necklace if you need me."

"How could I forget that?" My magical necklace had the ability to summon my norn—a little trick that came in handy. I hugged her back before passing her on to Ull.

"Visit whenever you can, Elsker. We love being able to see you."

"You too, boy." With a wink at Olaug, she headed into the English night.

"Well, shall we?" Olaug gestured toward the library. It was the entrance to the secret chamber beneath Ýdalir.

"Might as well." Ull set his jaw. I knew he hated that I was going to be like him; the idea literally immobilized him. And I knew why—he'd seen an immeasurable amount of destruction as an assassin, and he knew changing me would make me vulnerable to attacks from jotuns, and bad elves, and evil sprites, and whatever else lived in the realms I'd only just learned existed. But at the same time, he understood it was the only way to save our worlds—and ourselves.

My fingers grazed Ull's biceps and I gave him a questioning look. He took a breath. With a nod, he put his hand on the small of my back and guided me down the hall. There was no more putting it off. It was time to learn about my new job as Goddess of Winter.

We entered the library, and Olaug pulled the trigger-book from the shelf. A wall swung open, and we descended the golden-carpeted staircase that led underneath Ýdalir. The walls were paneled with a dark wood and lit with glowing sconces. A single room was nestled at the bottom of the path. There was an open kitchen on the left, well stocked with Ull's favorite coffees, teas, and snacks, so he could work uninterrupted. Straight ahead was a conference table underneath the enormous screen that beamed transmissions from Asgard. Dark leather couches were off to the right, and a network of laptops and scanners took up the corner space. And lining the far end of the chamber was a homage to Ull's past—bows, arrows, armor, skis, skates and snowshoes were kept safe in mahogany cases and locked behind glass doors.

This was Ull's private workspace.

"Ull, are you comfortable being down here while I teach Kristia?" Olaug walked past the kitchen area, glancing over her shoulder as she moved.

"I still do not feel right putting Kristia in danger. And if there were any other option, believe me, I would take it. But somebody is after her—he has been popping into her visions since I came into her life. And he wants to hurt her." Ull sounded haunted. "I need you to do everything in your power to put her in a position to protect herself."

Olaug seated herself in one of the leather chairs under Ull's armor while I made my way around the room, slowly eyeing the unfamiliar objects. Swords, skis, metal helmets . . . I was too keyed up to sit, knowing I was finally going to learn what my new life would be like.

"Then we have no time to waste." With that, Olaug started her lesson. "Kristia dear, I do not know what you have been told, so I shall start at the beginning."

And she did, with the stories I heard in my childhood and the ones I learned throughout my education. But the tales she told were more colorful, warmer, and more personal, and it was clear these mythological characters were real people—Ull's family, soon to be my own.

"The first rule of Asgard," Olaug began, "is *aldri endre*—things never change. The realms are in constant flux, the warriors engaged in perpetual battle, but all of these events were laid out long before our creation. They are premeditated, and in that sense, they are unvarying.

"Things change but they don't change?"

"Look at the history of our battles. Starting with creation: Odin and his brothers slayed the first jotun, Ymir. His body bled so terribly it caused a flood, killing all but two of the surviving jotun. They repopulated their race, and within years led an uprising against our people. Asgard quelled the insurgence, only to be faced with the first fire giant rebellion. After the fire giants came the dark elves, and so on. There has never been a time of peace in Asgard lasting more than a few hundred years."

"That seems like a long time," I pointed out.

"To you, yes." Olaug shook her head. "But from an immortal perspective, a hundred years passes in the blink of an eye. Our warriors are always training, always preparing for the next fight. In a very literal sense, Asgard can never let down its guard. And there are many who believe this is the way it will always be, simply because The Fates have decreed it."

My eyes sought out Ull's. He gave a small nod.

"Now, what was the first rule of Asgard?" Olaug quizzed.

"Don't talk about Asgard," I deadpanned.

Ull chuckled.

"The first rule of Asgard is things don't change," I amended.

They preached that up and down both ways 'til Sunday like it was Norse gospel. The muscles in my face fought against a simmering eye roll. *Like heck things didn't change.* I was walking proof Asgard's precious prophecies could be turned on their routine-loving heads.

Olaug watched my internal struggle with barely contained glee. "And how do you feel about that rule?"

"It's as wrong as a rooster in a china shop."

Ull shot me a glance. "Do you mean a bull in a china shop?"

"Nope. Rooster. Happened once in Nehalem. Well, the dishware section of the general store, but close enough. It was total chaos."

Ull stared.

"It was just bad all around. And so is this silly rule. No offense. If nothing ever changed, you wouldn't have come to earth, Ull. We wouldn't be together. Your dad wouldn't have agreed to change me. The Norns wouldn't have picked a human to do a god's job. Of course things change—that's just a part of living. Who made up that ridiculous rule, anyway?"

Ull glanced at Olaug. "Odin."

"Well, he's dead wrong, bless his heart. According to Asgard, Ragnarok's going to be the end of us, right? Nothing against your prophets, but I, for one, do not intend to die just because some fortune tellers and your grandpa say so."

Ull put his hands on my shoulders. The pads of his fingers stroked a firm line to the base of my skull, releasing the tension that built as I made my speech. His hands were *amazing*. "But you realize it is possible, no? That much as we fight against them, The Fates might know our destinies better than we do?"

I reached over to cup Ull's face in my hands. The prickle of his five o'clock shadow rubbed against my palms. My eyes caught his in a determined stare—maybe if I looked deeply enough, I could project the confidence I desperately needed him to have in us. "Ull. Did it ever occur to you that sometimes finding your destiny means doing the exact opposite of what The Fates have in store?"

Ull blinked at me. The blue of his eyes narrowed as his pupils dilated, absorbing a message that clearly had never occurred to him. To the consummate rule-follower, bucking the Asgardian system must have sounded stranger than a two-tailed mallard. I squeezed his hands, touching my forehead to his.

"Just think about it," I whispered.

"She is right." Olaug nodded. "We have Helheim, Nifhel, Jotunheim, Muspelheim and Svartalfheim fighting against us. Our enemies have attacked before, but never as a unified front. If we are to survive, we cannot afford to act as we always have. Whatever it is that Kristia is meant to be to us, she will be the one to bring about change."

"I do not like it." Ull shook his head. "But I know I cannot stop her."

"No," Olaug spoke softly. "You can't."

Ull wrapped an arm around my waist and guided me to the couch. I curled up against him, letting my hair fall across his chest as I lay my head on the fabric of his sweater. The contrast of hard muscle and soft cashmere was so *Ull*. It made me calm, despite my nerves.

"Why don't we tell her more about our relationship, Ull?" Olaug offered.

With his arm slung around me, Ull slid his massive hand over my abdomen. He rubbed slow circles across my flat stomach, resting his chin on the top of my head as he spoke. "Olaug is more than my grandmother. She acts as my link to Asgard. When Svartalfheim attacked the Dark Forest, Odin was hesitant to allow me to leave the realm. He agreed on the condition that Olaug join me.

"She runs official operations from Ýdalir, and relays messages as needed. Meanwhile I am able to delegate a portion of my duties to colleagues back home, and still tend to the most urgent issues from here. Telecommuting, so to speak."

"A modern god for a modern time." My cough poorly disguised my laughter.

"Always glad to be able to amuse you."

"I love you, Ull." I gazed up at him.

"Those are just words." He kissed my forehead. "When I am needed, Odin summons me through Olaug. We installed a portal to the Bifrost when we built Ýdalir."

"The Bifrost is the rainbow bridge that connects the realms to Asgard." I remembered.

"Correct. It is guarded by Heimdall. When called, he sends the bridge to the portal so we can return to Asgard, or visit another realm."

"So you literally walk on rainbows?" My mouth fell open just a little.

Ull shrugged. "It is not a big deal."

"Says the guy who walks on rainbows," I muttered. "And doesn't look a day over twenty. How do you all avoid aging? Is that a genetic god-thing, or do you take a vitamin or something?"

Olaug chuckled. "We eat apples."

"Pardon?" An apple a day was only supposed to keep the doctor away, not double for the fountain of youth.

"Apples," she repeated. "Our Goddess of Wisdom, Idunn, formulated a magical apple that slows the aging process. So long as we continue to eat the apples, our progression is delayed over a thousand percent. We do grow older, obviously." She held out one wrinkled hand. "But as Idunn continues to tinker with the formula, our life expectancies continue to increase. We have not had a god die of old age since she produced her first crop."

Unbelievable.

"If I eat them do I stay young too?"

"Not as you are. They do not have the same effect on mortals," Olaug explained.

"Apples. Who knew?" I fingered my necklace.

"Did you never wonder about all the apple pastries around Ýdalir?" Ull asked.

"I just thought you guys were really, really wholesome. Apple pie and all." I shrugged feebly.

"Oh, sweetheart." Ull patted my stomach.

"What? It's not a huge stretch. You *are* wholesome. I've never heard you swear."

Ull raised an eyebrow and pressed his lips to my ear. His cool breath made me shiver when he spoke. "Oh, you will," he promised.

Images of our imminent honeymoon flashed in my

head. Beads of sweat trickled down my neck. *Oh, Lord.*

"Now, Kristia," Olaug continued in her matronly tone, "the ceremony elevating you to Asgard can happen during your matrimony."

"How does it work, exactly?" The butterflies in my belly took flight.

"It is fairly simple." Olaug paused.

Ull listened intently since he didn't know how the conversion was going to happen either. No mortal had ever been allowed to become a god. I was something of a novelty.

"There will be a bit of prep work beforehand. Idunn will prepare your body for the transition to immortality." Olaug's eyes glazed. I sensed there was something she wasn't telling me, but she moved on quickly. "The formal transformation will occur at your wedding. Odin will raise Mjölnir above your head and sing an incantation affirming your worthiness while calling on the powers of Asgard. You will both give your assent and pledge your fealty to our realm, and it will be done."

"That's it?" I was incredulous. I thought for sure there would be spells and blades, the whole *eye of newt* thing. All we had to do was say some words under a hammer?

"Besides the preparation, that is all. Getting Odin's permission was the hard part. The ceremony itself is relatively simple." There it was again—that glazed look. I could guess at its meaning.

"Will it hurt?" I wasn't so good with pain. Flu shots were my undoing.

"Oh." Olaug chuckled. "I do not think so. No human has ever entered Asgard, so we are not entirely sure how this will go. But it should be fairly easy."

Talking about pain reminded me of something. "What about, well, fighting? Who's going to teach me?" Surely Olaug wasn't expected to cover that, too. I lobbed a hopeful face at Asgard's fiercest assassin, but he shook his head.

"I do not want you engaged in combat, Kristia. It is too risky."

"Elfie's come after me too many times. We both know I'll get attacked again."

"Your necklace has protected you in my place. As the Seer, you can channel Mjölnir's powers through it. I expect you to wear it at all times. And if the creature appears again, I want you to grab that necklace immediately; do not engage him in conversation. Do not ask him any questions. Do not try to fight him. Just grab the hammer, and get out of there."

"Ull—"

"I mean it, Kristia." It was a tone I didn't hear often. But I wasn't too concerned—I knew Ull's anger was just a mask for his fear.

I put my hands on both sides of his face. I stared him in the eye and took a deep breath. "I get that you're scared. I do. I'd freak out if I thought too hard about the things you do when you're dealing with warrior stuff. I'd be absolutely lost if anything ever happened to you."

"Kristia—"

"No, listen to me. I want us to talk this out and

move on, because we can't keep coming back to it." I made sure to keep my voice level.

"Fine. I do not want you fighting."

"I don't want me fighting, either. I want us laying on a beach somewhere, sipping fruity drinks and doing something a lot more fun than thinking about the Norse apocalypse."

"We agree on that." Ull smiled through his worry lines.

"So we want the same thing?" I traced his cheekbone with my finger. "We just have to figure out how to get there. And before we do, the odds are pretty good someone's going to come after me again—if not the elf, then someone else who'll want to use my visions. It's only a matter of time."

"What are you saying?" I felt Ull's jaw tense beneath my hand. I rubbed the muscles with my thumb.

"I'm saying that you have to give me a shot at protecting myself. Or you really might lose me. Forever."

Ull's face froze. He held himself perfectly still as a tremor passed through his body. Then he exhaled sharply and grasped both of my hands in his.

"I know," he whispered. He leaned down so his forehead rested against mine. "I am afraid for you."

"I'm kind of afraid for me, too. But you know what?" I lifted his chin with one finger and looked him in the eye.

"What?"

"I've got an awfully good fighter to show me the

ropes."

Ull cracked first. "You really want me to teach you?"

"I do. And it doesn't have to be now. It doesn't even have to be before the wedding. Just promise me you'll be the one to give me the tools I need to take care of myself. Because I want us to be together forever, and I don't need any giants kidnapping me or elves trying to off me again."

"All right." Ull closed his eyes. "I will do it. But you have to promise something in return."

"Okay."

Ull squeezed my hands and opened his eyes. "Promise you will not throw a fit when we arrange for your bodyguard."

"My what?" I took a step back and put my hands on my hips.

"Once your identity gets out, the line of creatures waiting to kidnap you will stretch from one end of the cosmos to the other. As the Seer, Odin will require you have twenty-four-hour detail."

"Absolutely not. No. I don't want some stranger following me around all the time. I already have you asking about my every vision. I'm covered." The idea of two overprotective-Ulls was too much.

"Sweetheart." Ull stepped forward and pulled me into his arms. I softened into him just a smidge, but I kept my hands firmly on my hips. "This is not about me. You are my world, yes. But as our visionary, you are also of tremendous value to Asgard. Odin will not let you roam the realms unsupervised. He is going to require security detail to keep you safe."

"Well, you're an assassin, right? Can't you do it?" I tried to squirm away, but Ull was so strong it was as if I were trying to wrestle a grizzly. I gave up and rested my cheek on his ribcage.

"I will protect you, yes. But at the end of the day, you are still going to need a bodyguard." He stroked the small of my back and I shivered. Without thinking, I dropped my hands from my hips and wrapped them around his waist.

"And if I promise not to freak out when I get this stalker—"

"Bodyguard," Ull corrected.

"Whatever. If I don't freak out, then you'll teach me to fight?"

"That is my offer, yes."

"Fine." I dropped my arms. Ull ran his hands over my hips and kissed the top of my head.

"Thank you, darling," he murmured into my hair.

"You're welcome," I muttered. "But you'd better teach me some really good moves."

"Oh, I plan to." His husky voice absolutely dripped with double meaning. I turned beet red.

"That's settled. Now can we get back to our lesson?" Olaug tapped her foot from across the room, and I buried my face in Ull's chest.

"Yes." Ull kissed my forehead and guided me back to the couches. I curled up against him and stroked his palm with the pads of my fingers. He slung his other arm comfortably around my shoulders and pulled me close.

Olaug smoothly steered the conversation toward my duties. "As Ull's wife you will be Goddess of Winter. As time goes on you may choose to take on additional responsibilities. That shall be at your discretion."

"But what will be expected of me as a . . . ." It was still weird to say *goddess* out loud. "As one of you?"

"Not much at first, my dear," Olaug reassured me. "Everyone wants to see you have an easy transition." Ull looked up. "I spoke with Sif just before you arrived. She says 'hello,' and 'why don't you visit more?'"

Ull laughed. "Typical." His fingertips rubbed soft circles on my arm and a slow burn built on my skin. My pulse spiked, but the proximity of Ull's grandmother helped ebb the hormones.

"She is very excited for your wedding. She never thought she would see the day," Olaug teased gently. "Neither did I. We are all so happy you have come along, Kristia. You are the blessing none of us knew to ask for."

"Agreed." Ull brushed his lips against my hair.

"Thank you." I felt the heat race across my cheeks.

"Would you ladies care for tea?" Ull asked.

"Yes, please." I kissed his bottom lip and Ull headed to the kitchen to make a fresh pot.

"So when are you going to teach me how to, you know, manage my—" I broke off and signed a circle by my ear, the universal sign for "crazy." I could not wait to have some control over my handicap.

"I am afraid there is not much you can do until after you have been changed," Olaug responded. "You will not have the strength of Asgard until then. And trying to channel your powers without it would be dangerous. If you were separated from your body in the tenth realm—"

"Olaug!" Ull set the kettle down with a little too much force.

"She is going to find out about it soon enough."

"The tenth realm? No, there are nine. Asgard, Vanaheim, Alfheim, Svartalfheim, Jotunheim, Nidavellir, Nifhelm, Muspelheim and . . . oh. Midgard." I ticked them off by rote. One started paying a *lot* more attention in Professor Carnicke's mythology class when one found out one's boyfriend was a living, breathing Norse deity.

Olaug stared at Ull. "Do you want to tell her or should I?"

I watched the vein on Ull's neck bulge until I was pretty sure it was going to burst. "It's okay. I can just find out later."

Ull let out one long breath. He eyed me levelly, as if he were waiting for me to run away.

"Ull? What's wrong?"

"I do not know how much more I can subject you to," he admitted. "This is not a small matter."

"Try me."

Ull nodded. He set down a silver serving-tray with teacups, milk, sugar and spoons. When he was done, he stared at me with a guarded expression. "There is another plane beyond the nine realms—an alternate reality you can visit to obtain information. A tenth realm."

CHAPTER THREE

"THERE'S AN ALTERNATE REALITY? Like, a parallel universe?" I squeaked. That sounded absurd. Though, given the origins of my company, I probably should have been beyond surprises.

"It is simply another place you can send a part of your spirit for a term. Another realm that has . . . . special powers," Ull explained.

"You can send your spirit to another realm?" The words tumbled out of my mouth before I could stop them. "You can separate yourself from your spirit? Actually cut out your soul? Like in a horror movie?"

"No, nothing like that," Olaug assured me just as Ull nodded.

"Well, which is it?" I croaked.

Ull and Olaug exchanged a look. Ull spoke first. "Yes, you can separate yourself from your spirit. Send it on a journey your physical body cannot make. No, you are not cutting out your soul—the spirit will return to your body, provided you keep it intact in the tenth realm."

"And no, it is nothing like a horror movie," Olaug assured me. "It is reasonably painless, or so I'm told. I've never actually done it before."

"You haven't? And you think I'm going to be able to?" There was no disguising the panic from my voice.

"I *know* you are going to be able to," Olaug promised. If only I could feel half as confident as she sounded. "Elsker will train you. Extensively. When the time comes, you will be more than ready."

"You can actually send your spirit to another realm?" There were so many things that could go wrong in that scenario. First of all, how did you get your spirit out of your body? And once it was away from your brain, how did you tell it where to go and what to do? What happened if it decided it wanted its independence and went off on a European cruise, leaving your body spirit-less? This could be a total debacle. What if . . . *Oh my God*. "What if Elfie finds me? My body lying spiritless, or my spirit off in Never-Never Land? What would happen to me?"

The vein in Ull's neck bulged. His square jaw worked itself back and forth before setting in a firm line.

"It's that bad?" My mouth was so dry, my tongue felt like someone had glued it to my teeth.

"I promised I would not let anything bad happen to you, Kristia. But you have to understand that if you choose to do this, if you choose to enter the tenth realm, there is a possibility I will not be able to protect you. If I were to travel with you, your body would be left unattended. And if I stay with your body, I cannot be with your spirit. I cannot protect both parts of you if you separate them from one another. But the thought of not being able to take care of any part of you absolutely terrifies me."

In that instant I understood why Ull looked so angry. I'd put him in an impossible position. He planned for every possible outcome when it came to my safety: bodyguards and babysitters, and a carefully orchestrated training regimen to guide me into his world. He walked me to school most days, checked to make sure I was in my flat every night before he went to sleep, and just *happened* to show up any time I stayed late at the library. In an ordinary boyfriend it would have been cloying, but there was nothing ordinary about Ull. He'd seen, and dealt, fatal blows to more than one immortal. He knew how very fragile my mortality would make me in his world. But at the same time, every step closer to my becoming a god meant we were a step closer to Ull's worst fear coming true—having me in a situation he couldn't control.

And here I was, throwing the thing that terrified him the most right in his face.

For the first time, I wondered if I'd made a mistake. Maybe going through with this wasn't the right thing to do. If severing my soul, even to stop Ragnarok, would cause Ull this much worry, then maybe I wasn't looking out for him at all. Maybe I was being selfish. But what choice did I have? If I didn't do the job The Fates had unwittingly assigned me, Ragnarok would mark the end of our worlds. It wasn't like we had a whole lot of options.

I'd asked what would happen if Elfie found my body or my spirit alone. Ull's reaction had given me my answer. But at the end of the day, the question was moot. Ull had become my entire reason for being. He was so concerned with taking care of me that he didn't realize that I was set on doing the same for him. Not even the very real likelihood of my death would stop me from doing everything I could do to protect him from Ragnarok.

I crossed the room in quick strides. My fingers grazed the taut muscles of Ull's chest as I rested my head on his torso. Strong arms wrapped around my lower back, pulling me into the embrace I knew I could never live without. "I'm sorry. I really am. If there were another way to do this, you know I would. But there's a lot riding on my pulling this off. Our realms need me—"

"I need you," Ull growled.

"I need you too." My lips moved against his bicep. "More than you'll ever know. And I promise I'm not going to leave you. Ever. No matter what I have to do as this Seer person. You're stuck with me. You have to believe in this; in us."

"I want to." Ull looked haunted.

"That's good enough for now." I stood on my tiptoes to kiss his cheek. "Now this spirit-splitting trick—is it a god thing?" Surely no mortal had ever done something so magical.

"No." Ull went back to preparing the tea. "Humans could visit the tenth realm, with proper training. But few have the necessary discipline to do it safely."

"So it's something I could do now? Before you change me?" My desperation to get some kind of control over my mental handicap crawled over my concern for Ull's feelings like the feral squirrel that lived behind the Nehalem General Store. That thing was vicious.

"Absolutely not. Sending your spirit to the plane is risky enough for a mortal, but for someone of your abilities . . . . Kristia, if our enemies got wind that the Seer sent her unprotected spirit—" Ull exhaled sharply. "They could kidnap that part of you. You would be incomplete, and they would have control over your powers. I do not want to think about what they could do to you."

"But Ull, if there's anything I can do to help your family . . ."

Ull gripped the handle of the teapot so tightly his knuckles cracked.

"Kristia," Olaug interrupted gently. "It isn't a good idea for you to try anything of this magnitude while you are mortal. You are too valuable to the realm to take that risk. Much is resting on you."

"There has to be *something* I can do now. I feel so helpless."

"Well, it would fall strictly under Elsker's purview," Olaug hesitated. "But maybe she and I could at least explain to you how the visions will work once you have access to the alternate realm. Now, I don't want you attempting to separate from your body, understand that. But we can give you a bit of an overview of how the process will work, so you can mentally prepare yourself."

"That would be great." *Anything to quell this feeling of being totally useless in the face of an impending apocalypse.* "Thanks."

The sound of grinding teeth came from my betrothed.

"I promised I would prepare her, Ull. You must allow me to do the job you asked me to do," Olaug pointed out.

"I know," Ull grunted. "But I get to be here when you work."

"Oh, no. I cannot adequately prepare her with you glaring over my shoulder." Olaug planted a hand on her waist. I eyed Ull warily. He was definitely glaring. Was there any way to circumvent his overprotective nature and let Olaug work in peace?

I rubbed at my temples as a barrage of needles pounded inside my head. As quickly as it had come the pain passed, but in the interim I'd had an insight. Lovely. If I tried to force the visions, I got a migraine.

No matter. I pushed through the discomfort. "Okay. Ull is going to start taking long walks alone to think about Ragnarok. He won't want me to see how worried he is, so he'll go off by himself for about an hour every week."

"Why are you talking about me as if I am not here?" Ull crossed his arms.

"How do you know this?" Olaug ignored the irritated idol behind her.

I tapped my head. "I had another vision."

"Oh, all right. I will speak with Elsker. If she

approves then the three of us shall talk—talk only, Kristia—about your visions when Ull takes his walks."

"I am not planning to take any walks," Ull declared.

"You will."

"This is going to be beyond irritating," Ull muttered.

"You're stuck with me now."

He knew I had him there.

* * * *

When I stifled my third yawn of the evening, we retreated to the upstairs kitchen for waffles. I was exhausted, as I knew my companions would be too, if not for their super-human abilities. Olaug stayed to eat with us, then began the short walk across the way to her own home. When she had gone, Ull and I sat on the porch swing in the garden, listening to the nightingales. The low, stone path was lined with white roses and lavender, and Ull had left the twinkling lights up in the ancient yew dale. They were a nice touch.

"What a day." My voice was barely a whisper as Ull rubbed my shoulders. Everything was so peaceful. I didn't want to break the evening's spell.

"Is this too much? You do not have to do this. We—"

I silenced him with a finger to his lips. "It *is* too much."

A tense line formed between Ull's eyebrows. "I knew it. Listen, you have another option. There is a safe house in every quadrant of your realm. We can go to one, live out our lives as mortals. Nobody outside

Odin's council knows the safe houses exist, so I can promise you absolute security."

"Until the wolf and the snake get hungry and Ragnarok kicks off." I shook my head. "You didn't let me finish. This *is* too much—learning about thousands of years of attacks on your realm; hearing all the ways I could, and very likely will, die; finding out I'm going to do some weird soul-splitting exercise that's going to leave me completely exposed to Elfie . . . it's complete and total madness."

"I will take you away right now." Ull rose to his feet. He took a step toward the cottage, but I grabbed his wrist and pulled him back. He fell onto the swing with a heavy thud, eyebrows raised and mouth hanging open. "Kristia!"

"Let me finish." I repeated. "It's *way* too much—but I always knew it would be. I walked into this deal with my eyes open. You don't get engaged to an actual Norse god without expecting some rough patches. For better or worse, right?"

Ull closed his eyes. "My 'worse' is not exactly the run-of-the-mill marital problem."

"I know that." I twined my fingers through his hair and swung my legs across his lap. He wrapped one arm around me from behind. The slow burn ebbing across my backside traveled down my legs, leaving a tingling sensation from hip to toe. *The things this god could do to me . . .*

"I want so much better for you than the life I am able to offer." Ull brushed his lips against my ear. "I want to give you the universe. Instead, I am asking you to risk your life. It is not fair."

"Life's not fair," I repeated his long-ago words. "And that's okay with me. You, Ull Myhr, are a god worth risking it all for."

"I want more for you," Ull breathed into my ear.

"You are my more." I turned so our lips were nearly touching. My nose brushed against his as I gazed up into the face that held my confidences, hopes, and fears in one delicious, heart-stopping package. "And I'm more than willing to take this on. I don't care what happens to me in that tenth realm. Our worlds are on the brink of war, and I'm going to do everything I can to make sure you and I have a shot at our happy-ever-after. I'm doing this for our family. I'm doing this for *us*. And when it's over, you're going to take me to that safe house, turn off your phone, and ignore Odin, or Heimdall, or Santa Claus, or whoever else you do business with for a *very* long time." I kissed his bottom lip, running my tongue over the pale flesh. He tasted like lingonberry jam and waffles: savory. Tart. Amazing.

"Are you certain?" Ull murmured, his tongue moving against mine. For a moment I indulged in the sensations Ull stirred in me. I took his lip between my teeth, tugging gently as I pulled my head back. He let out a groan and hiked me up on his lap, squeezing my behind as he did. My fingers gripped his hair, blond silky strands wrapping around the diamonds in my ring. I pulled his mouth back to mine, warm tongues and soft lips moving together. I could have stayed right there forever.

With a heavy breath, Ull gently lifted me off his lap. He set me down on the bench beside him and cupped my cheek with one hand. "Are you certain?"

My fingers brushed the stubble of his cheek as I fought to remember what exactly I was supposed to be certain of. Oh. Right. Imminent death for the sake of our future. *No problem*. "I've never been more sure of anything. I want to be your equal in every way. And being your partner, helping you . . . it's going to be amazing." I pulled my finger back and kissed him gently, then nuzzled my head into the crook of his neck.

Ull lifted my chin with a finger. "What are you feeling?"

"Happy." I gazed into his endless eyes.

"I mean, what are you feeling about all of this? Becoming a goddess? Fighting for Asgard?"

"I'm a little nervous," I answered honestly. "I don't know if I'm strong enough to be of any use to your family. I don't want to let you down."

"You could never, my love. You have no idea what it means that you would take all of this on for me. But you must know that you do not have to do this. I do not want you to be afraid."

"I would do anything for you."

"And I for you."

Ull lowered his mouth to mine. I breathed in his woodsy scent and parted my lips, inviting him back in. He reached up to caress my hair. I wrapped my fingers around the collar of his sweater and pulled myself closer. He groaned, and this time the sound was too much. I climbed onto his lap and nestled against him, relishing the feel of his muscles against my torso. He grabbed my head and leaned me back in the swing, supporting me with his arm. He held me at an angle, kissing me with such purpose my brain was quickly devoid of oxygen.

"Ull," I panted. I wished more than anything I didn't have to breathe. Ull pulled back, disheveled hair falling to his cheekbones and desire burning in his eyes.

"Kristia Tostenson," he growled softly. "I don't know what I did to deserve you, but I am the luckiest god alive."

He righted me, carefully tucking me under one arm. I brushed my face against his cashmere sweater and smiled. I couldn't help but feel lucky, too.

❄❄❄❄

"So you really don't need anything? Anything at all?" My best friend sounded incredulous.

"Honest, Ardis. We're good." I sat on the guest bed at Ýdalir with my manicure kit spread before me. I tucked my phone between my ear and my shoulder as I used a cotton swab to remove my nail polish. Since I'd started wearing Ull's ring, I'd taken a *lot* more interest in the state of my nails.

"You don't need me to comb through wedding websites with you? Maybe help pick out flowers? Peonies are *huge* this season."

"How do you know that? Are you reading wedding magazines? Because I'm pretty sure that's what the cover of Emma's new one said."

"I might have picked up a few since you got engaged," Ardis admitted. "What? Those suckers are addictive!"

"Apparently." I laughed. "Victoria and Emma are still buying them every week from our corner market. They're not even pretending they're for me at this point. I hardly ever look at them."

"Why not? Aren't you excited about your wedding?"

"Of course I am! I'm excited about *our* wedding. The simple little ceremony we're having for our immediate family and best friends. No magazines required." I could picture Ardis tugging on her lip on the other end of the line.

"Who's going with you to try on dresses?" she demanded.

"I'm wearing my grandmother's dress," I reminded her. "Olaug is going to make a bouquet of roses from the garden. And Inga's taking care of the stuff Ull and I don't care about, like the cake and the decorations."

"Who doesn't care about her own wedding decorations?" Ardis sounded perplexed.

I laughed.

"No, I get it. This is you. You see the big picture and don't get bogged down by the little things. You've always been like that." Ardis sighed. "I'm so excited for you, Kristia. Life wasn't easy on you growing up. You deserve a happy ending."

"I don't know how much I deserve this. But I'm sure as daylight grateful I get to marry Ull." I slicked a glossy base coat over my pinky.

"Sounds like he's one in a million." I could hear my friend's smile.

"You have no idea," I mumbled. "So what about you? Are you seeing anyone new?"

Ardis launched into a story about the three dates she'd been on that week. I settled into the pillows and giggled as I waited for my nails to dry. We might have been different as night and day, but I missed my best friend like crazy. I absolutely couldn't wait to see her at the wedding.

❄ ❄ ❄ ❄

Cold air pushed past my face as I tumbled through the darkness. It whipped my silk pajama bottoms against my legs, the thin fabric offering little protection against the chill. My fingernails dug into my bare arms in a pointless effort to still the goose pimples. I fell in slow motion, a kind of measured traverse, making my way down a black chasm.

When I accepted I might never stop this unending descent, my body jerked upward. It hovered in the abyss, weightless and waiting. After an interminable moment, I heard a loud snap. It sounded like a clap of thunder, or the slam of a nearby door. Whatever it was, it put an end to the purgatory. I dropped to the ground, landing feet-first in what appeared to be a forest. It had the requisite trees, but everything was a little bit off—like I was seeing things through a looking glass. The trees were taller than I was used to—redwood giants like the ones back home, but instead of green moss growing around their trunks these were cloaked in purplish leaves. They stretched thirty feet upward from the thick roots, forming a checkerboard pattern along the lush bark. The ground was swathed in vegetation, weaving a tapestry from the ground where I stood to a grey stone wall. Over the top of the wall I could see a structure of connected towers and spires—a castle? A cacophony of grunts came from within the castle walls. Whoever was on the other side was engaged in intense physical activity. Something told me it wasn't lawn bowling.

Where had my mental tic taken me now?

I scanned the area between the trees and the wall. It was empty, save for the peculiar plants and a cluster of oversized rocks. An unnaturally large bird circled overhead; it was easily the size of a small truck. It traced a path across the ginger sky. Was it dawn? Dusk? I'd never seen the sky quite that color before.

My eyes followed the bird as it flew over the castle wall. When it crossed the plane, an arrow shot from somewhere in the courtyard. It arced toward the animal fast as a fiddle, and pierced the bird just as it was about to land on one of the towers. The bird bucked at the impact. With wings still mid-flap, it spiraled down to the ground where it landed with a thud loud as a fallen sequoia.

"Arkeya!" *Came the cry from inside the wall. The deafening pounding of feet alerted me to the number of occupants in the courtyard. There must have been a hundred people in there. I crept toward the wall, my head swiveling back and forth to make sure I wasn't being watched. But save for the bird that didn't make it, I hadn't actually seen another living being.*

What was this place?

The wall must have been twenty-feet high—scaling it unnoticed would have been a tall order for a girl who'd never been accused of being the most graceful goose in the gaggle. But after a bit of searching I found a stone with a chunk missing. It was at calf level, and I crawled until my eye was even with the small opening. I squinted through the hole, wondering how much falling through the black hole had messed with my head. There was no way what my eyes were seeing was any sort of reality.

Inside the courtyard stood not one hundred, but only two-dozen massive creatures. They looked human enough, except for their unkempt hair, boil-ridden skin, and their absolutely massive size. Each one stood twenty-five-feet tall, maybe higher, with arms that dwarfed the trunks of the redwoods and calves easily twice that girth. They were huddled around the fallen truck-bird, ripping pieces of meat from its body and shoving it in their mouths. The sickening crunch of teeth on bone set my ears on edge. As I watched, one pulled a piece of cartilage from his mouth and threw it over his shoulder. It landed directly in front of my peephole; bloody tendons slapped against the wall, temporarily obscuring my vision.

Ew.

With a flourish, the creature holding a bow plunged his hand into the bird's chest cavity. There was a gurgling sound as blood rushed out of the animal. Then the creature withdrew his hand, holding aloft the bird's lifeless heart. He let out another cry, then shoved the heart into his mouth. He bit down, grinning as blood dripped over his lips and onto his enormous hands. He wiped them across the fabric of his strangely fitted robe, streaks of crimson staining the yellowing fabric.

My gut heaved as I doubled over, emptying the contents of my stomach onto the dirt. The hairs on the back of my neck stood on end while I prayed my outburst hadn't outed my location. Whatever those creatures were, they weren't friendly. They'd taken down a bird that probably out-weighed me by a few hundred pounds. Who knew what they'd do if they found me on the other side of their wall?

I was psyching myself up to make a run for the forest when I heard the voice. Smooth. Low. Simultaneously grating and sexy.

Elfie.

I knew Ull would have wanted me to grip my necklace and get out of Dodge. But curiosity clutched me by the hand and dragged me back to the peephole. I pressed my eye to the space in the stone as the slick voice called from inside the courtyard.

"Friends."

Elf Man stood in the center of the square, arms out and head high. Unlike the creatures in their strange robes, he wore plain clothes—slim-fitting black jeans, and a loose black shirt. His hair was slicked back, and his calculating eyes shot sparks. He was here on a mission, and he was determined.

"Ara galough." *One of the creatures crouched down. His head lowered as if he were about to charge.*

"I come in peace." Elfie held up his hands. "Can anyone tell me where I might find Surtr? I brought a gift

for your king." He held out a package.

"Here," a guttural voice barked. Another creature emerged from the castle, but this one wore long purple robes caked in sparkling stones. Light bounced off their mottled green surface, projecting patterns onto the courtyard walls with each step. "Why have you come?"

"Ah, Your Excellency." Elfie dropped to one knee. He bowed his head, holding the package out with both hands. Surtr crossed the courtyard slowly, one leg dragging slightly behind the other. When he reached Elfie he took the gift. Elfie bowed his head as he drew himself up before the monarch. He clasped his hands in front of his waist. When he looked up, his face bore a terrifying grin. "I've come to share the most glorious news."

"Well?" Surtr didn't mince words.

"The Norns have seen the fall of Asgard. It is nearly time. But I need the strength of the fire giants to ensure nothing disrupts my little war."

"You want me to fight your battle for you?" Surtr grunted.

"No, my liege. I want you to fight it with me. You are the last piece of my puzzle—the proverbial checkmate to ensure the fall of our mutual enemy. Will you join my cause?"

"And risk the lives of the few men I have left? Odin's annihilation following the rebellion was practically genocide. I cannot afford to put my people at risk." Surtr shook his head. "You are on your own."

"I see." Elfie tapped his fingers together. "And I had so hoped . . . never mind."

"Hoped what?" Surtr crossed his arms over his chest.

"You see, Your Highness, I had hoped you would rule Midgard after the battle. With the chaos that will follow, I won't be able to handle the realms on my own. The female humans could assist in the repopulation of Muspelheim, and your constituents would have two realms at their disposal. But if you prefer to remain here, numbers depleted, food sources dwindling . . ." Elfie eyed the group of giants at the edge of the courtyard. Those who weren't crouched defensively toward him were still picking apart the truck-bird. Its meat was long gone; now they were chewing on bones.

"They are starving." Surtr stared at the scavengers. "Odin stripped the forest after the rebellion. The birds are all that is left."

"So terrible." Elfie clucked his tongue. "I don't know how you've managed all these years."

Surtr's eyes narrowed. "You are playing a game."

"I assure you, any game I play will only benefit you. I need brute strength to debilitate the gods. Without it, well . . . I hope I do not have to think about that possibility." Elfie held out a hand. "Do we have a deal? Will you help me?"

Surtr thought for a long moment. His eyes darted between the scavenging soldiers in the courtyard, and Elfie's outstretched palm. After a prolonged hesitation, he tucked the gift behind his back and shook Elfie's hand. "We have a deal. I will help you bring down the Aesir. And when we do, my people will avail themselves of Midgard and its resources."

"Precisely." Elf Man nodded at the gift, and Surtr shifted so he held it between them. "For you. Something for your guards to play with."

Surtr placed his hand in the box and withdrew a silver rod. He tilted it from side to side. The orange sun bounced an intricate pattern off the shiny surface, but other than that it looked like any ordinary rod. "What is this?"

"Aim it at the south wall," Elfie suggested. I pressed my face against the stone. Which direction was south? If the sun rose in the east and set in the west like it did on earth, then judging from the positioning of the orange orb overhead . . .

Oh, crimeny. I *was beyond the south wall. Elfie knew I was here the whole time. He was playing me . . . again. Which meant that little silver stick was going to—*

I jumped to my feet and bolted for the cover of the woods. The explosion came as soon as I started to run. Stones flew thirty feet in the air, breaking apart mid-flight and landing in a spray of shrapnel. I covered my head with my arms and fled, never stopping to assess the damage.

"There she is! Seize her!" Elfie's voice rang across the clearing. The sound of thundering footsteps echoed behind me as I ran a serpentine pattern through the redwoods. I stumbled on the oversized roots more than once, giving my pursuers time to close the distance between us.

I pumped my arms in a pointless effort to pick up speed. The balls of my feet burned as I pushed off them with every ounce of strength I had. But no sooner had I rounded a corner into a dense grove, then I heard the "whoosh" of fire and saw the blaze at my feet. Surtr had shot the silver rod directly at me . . . and now an inferno blazed in the forest. I turned away from the heat to run in another direction, but the fire closed its circle, encompassing me in a rapidly-shrinking cell.

My feet felt hotter than a desert in July. I glanced down and stomped at the fire. It was pointless—the flames were growing, and closing in on all sides. But I couldn't just stand there. I had to at least try to save myself.

"Sweet Kristia," Elf Man called from the other side of the fire. "Still think you can outwit me?"

I turned a slow circle, looking for any out. The ring of fire was shrinking around me. Within a minute it would swallow me up. This couldn't be happening.

"Pity, really. You could have been my crowning glory. My queen, perhaps. Who'd have thought Muspelheim would be your undoing? Such a waste." Elfie's laughter echoed off the trees. "See you in Helheim."

In that moment I knew it would never end—for whatever reason, I was his white whale. He'd chase me to the ends of the cosmos until he ended my life. And if I didn't learn to get a grip on these visions, I'd be handing myself right over.

My hand flew to the necklace that had saved me before. I should have used it to escape the minute I heard Elfie's voice, but I'd let myself get distracted. So stupid! I squeezed hard, willing it to work. When nothing happened I squeezed again. And again. The flames danced closer, lapping at the hems of my pajamas. I jumped back as the heat burned my ankle. With Elfie's cackles closing in from all sides, I gripped my necklace with both hands. Sending a silent prayer, I squeezed tightly.

And once again I was tumbling through a black abyss.

CHAPTER FOUR

WHEN I CAME TO, my chest heaved with sobs. Cold sweat cloaked my body from my forehead to the backs of my knees. My hair was damp, my pulse was racing, and my fingers gripped the sheets so tightly my knuckles ached. I was in my room at Ýdalir, the one place I had always felt safe. Only now I was absolutely terrified.

I ripped the covers off and wrapped my arms around my legs. My nose twitched at an unfamiliar smell. I pulled the cord on the bedside lamp, and looked around to see what might be burning. There was no smoke in the room; all of the furniture seemed to be intact. But when I glanced down, I saw the hems of my pajamas. They were black, singed from the fire I'd desperately hoped had been part of a dream.

This time things had gone too far. If my smoldering pant legs were any indication, being injured in a vision could have far-reaching worldly consequences. And if Elfie had come that close to killing me . . .

Ull had his rules, but I no longer cared. I jumped out of bed and raced down the hallway. When I reached his door I pounded on the distressed wood. Tears streamed down my face but I didn't bother to wipe them away. The downpour was too intense; it wouldn't have done any good anyway.

The door flew open and Ull stood on the other side. He wore a loose pair of grey sweatpants and nothing else. *Oh hot bejeebus.* There was no way this guy was for real. It just wasn't humanly possible to look that good.

Oh, right. Ull wasn't human.

Despite the agony coursing through my awakening consciousness, this was a moment of glory I'd remember forever—the first time I saw Ull's naked torso. His sweats hung low on his hips, affording me a view of the cut just above the bone.

Holy Lord.

"Kristia?" Ull rubbed the sleep from his eyes. He took in my matted hair, tear-streaked face, and shaking hands. "Great Odin. What happened?"

He pulled me to him, crushing my face against the muscles of his chest. The knot in my stomach loosened infinitesimally. Just being near Ull gave me peace, but being *this* near Ull was like taking a sedative. Breathing in his woodsy smell made my panic subside. And when he pressed his hands against me—one to my hair, the other against the small of my back—my gut knew I was safe. Nothing bad could happen to me so long as I was in Ull's arms. I inhaled again, letting his familiar scent fill me from the inside until my shaking stilled. Then I pressed my lips against his skin. Hard.

"Sweetheart?" he asked again.

"I had another vision and it freaked me out. Can I sleep here tonight?" I didn't take my lips off his chest as I spoke. I couldn't. He tasted divine—like spruce and soap and home. There was a very real possibility my mouth might be permanently adhered to his flesh, like a kid who'd tried to lick a frozen railing. Only this was far less unpleasant.

"Of course." Ull guided me to the king-sized sleigh bed. He helped me climb into it, tucking the downy comforter around my legs before crossing to the door. "I will be right back." He returned ten seconds later, and handed me a glass of water. "Drink," he ordered as he climbed into bed. I took a few sips before I put the glass on the nightstand. Between the terrifying vision, my singed PJ's, and the half-naked god in bed next to me, hydration was the furthest thing from my mind.

I was fixated on the spectacular planes of Ull's pecs, the deep ruts outlining each individual stomach muscle, and the angular line that ran on a diagonal from his ribcage toward his belly button. Obliques, I remembered memorizing in anatomy class. A light trail of hair ran down the center of his chest, ending somewhere beneath the elastic of his sweatpants. An involuntary whimper escaped my lips before I could stop it.

"Now tell me what happened." Ull rested his back against the headboard. He lifted me by my hips, nestling me against him. He pulled me back and wrapped his arms around me. The butterflies fluttered comfortably, now that we were in our happy place.

"I saw Elf Man again," I admitted. My fingers hooked around Ull's forearms and I squeezed my eyes shut to push out the image of the flame-throwing demon.

"Do you know where you were? Was it here?"

"No. We were with fire giants. He was talking to someone called Surtr."

"Their king?" Ull drew a sharp breath. "What did he say?"

I buried my head in Ull's ribcage.

"Oh, sweetheart." Ull stroked my arm. "It is okay. We do not have to relive it."

"They were talking about Elf Man's plan. Ull, he wants to destroy the gods—all the gods. I think he's the one orchestrating Ragnarok."

Ull's arms tensed under my fingers. I could feel the shallowness of his breaths as he attempted to calm himself. "What did he do to you?" The words were so clipped that I barely understood them.

"He tried to burn me," I admitted. "My pajamas got singed. But I'm okay—I grabbed my necklace and I came out of the vision. I'm sorry I woke you. I know you're exhausted, but—"

Ull silenced me with a finger to my lips. "Do not *ever* apologize for coming to me. I will *always* look out for you. Always. It is my duty and my honor."

I closed my eyes. "I was terrified."

"I bet you were. But you do not have to be afraid. I am here, and I will take care of you."

"He's going to kill everyone we know." My cheeks flushed as hot tears streamed down my face. "And then the fire giants are going to take over earth and eat us, or make us their slaves, or . . . I'm not sure. Either way, it's going to be awful!"

"Shh." Ull reached up to wipe the tears from my eyes. "I will not let that happen. Any of it. You are safe now."

"But I'm not!" I tilted my cheek into Ull's palm and sobbed. "There's nothing I can do to stop the visions. They just keep coming. And they're getting scarier and more real, and this time my pants were actually on fire. He's going to kill me, Ull. One way or another, this guy is going to hunt me down until he finally catches me. And then what am I going to do?"

I gave in to the panic I'd felt in the forest. Sobs wracked my body as I turned to face Ull. I cried until my throat was hoarse and my eyes burned, while Ull stroked my hair. He didn't try to reassure me, he didn't tell me to get a grip, and to his credit, he didn't ask me why I hadn't used my necklace to exit the vision the minute I'd realized I was in it . . . even though he'd asked me to do just that on several occasions. Instead he just held me and let me work through my fear.

When it was over, he lifted my chin with one finger. He wiped my eyes with the pads of his thumbs, and lay a gentle kiss on my forehead.

"Stay with me tonight," he commanded. "But know that we are going to find a way to stop him from getting into your head. And I am never, *never* going to let him hurt you. I vowed to protect you, and nothing is going to stop me from keeping my word. *Nothing.*"

"I'm scared, Ull."

"I know. I am uncomfortable with what happened tonight. But you are with me now, and I propose you never leave."

"Okay," I whispered. I buried my face in his chest. We lay together for a long while, the tension slowly evaporating into the high ceilings.

"I love you." Ull brushed my forehead with his lips.

"I love you, too." I kissed him back, my mouth warm on his chest.

In that moment something shifted. Ull brought the palm of his hand up to my bottom. He gave a gentle squeeze, and I lifted my head, curiosity getting the better of me. This wasn't like him—usually he was King of the Boundaries, and I'd expected our location would make him even more restrained. But the look in his eyes said differently. It was stern, searing, almost overwhelming in its longing.

It was sexy.

I threw myself on top of him and touched the hard muscles of his torso. Thick biceps wrapped around my arms, pinning me firmly in place. Ull's mouth found my chin for the briefest possible moment. His lips felt hot as he kissed a line down my neck to my shoulder. He nipped at the bone with his teeth, sending me spiraling down the side of a steep hill I hadn't realized I was standing on. As he kissed a trail to the hollow of my neck I fell faster, harder, adrenaline coursing through my veins and a thousand dormant nerve-endings springing to life. I sighed, giving in to the pulse of hormones pounding a rhythm against my skin. Ull's mouth found mine, and I lost myself all over again. But as much as my body wanted to stay where I was, my brain's need for oxygen prevailed; I pulled my head back with a gasp.

Ull stilled. He eyed me levelly, and very gently lifted me off him. He nestled me in the crook of his arm, and turned so he could place one hand on my stomach. He raised the fabric at the bottom of my thin camisole, and stroked soft circles on my belly with his thumb. My eyes rolled closed. Even this tiny touch was almost more than I could handle.

"You are to sleep here tonight. In the morning we will talk to Olaug about these visions. She and Elsker need to figure out how to help you block them. We know you can exit the visions using your necklace, but there must be some way to avoid them completely. I do not ever want you to come to my door crying again." He raised an eyebrow. "Although I do rather like you in my bed."

"I like it too," I confessed. "I feel safe here."

Ull nipped gently at my ear, once again giving me the not altogether uncomfortable feeling of spiraling out of my body. I inhaled deeply, then rested my cheek against his bare skin. No matter what had happened an hour ago, in this moment I was exactly where I wanted to be.

"Well then, sweetheart. This is where you shall stay."

❄❄❄❄

A few days later, I'd managed to push my latest nightmare to the back of my mind. Elsker had been less forgiving than Ull—she'd given me quite the lecture when she found out I stayed in the vision, even after I knew Elfie was there. When she stopped her tirade, she instructed me to grip my necklace and say her name *immediately* on entering a vision. I wasn't to engage the monster again, or listen in on his conversations—even though spying on him could give us valuable Ragnarok insight. For now my only job was to call for her. She promised she would come find me in whatever realm the vision took me to, and get me out. But her extraction would only work if she wasn't being detained. We both suspected Elf Man was working with a good-sized network of monsters, and in all likelihood any move he made to take me out would be preempted by debilitating my Norn. It was extremely clever. And even more terrifying.

With the visions under some theoretical semblance of control, I decided to blow off some steam with a girl's day.

"Are you going to tell me where we're going?" Inga's driving always made me nervous. Ull's super-hot roommate and second-oldest friend was good at a lot of things: baking, fashion, decorating, pretty much every sport, and keeping Ull's temper in check, but driving under the speed limit wasn't one of them. She took the winding turns out of Cardiff way too quickly, settling onto the motorway with a satisfied expression. My mind had finally wrapped itself around the fact that Norse gods were adrenaline junkies. My stomach was going to need more convincing.

"It should take about an hour to get there. I want to show you one of my favorite things about living as a human."

"I'd like to be a living human when we get there," I muttered.

"Ha, ha. Don't worry, I promised Ull I'd bring you home in one piece."

"Corpses come in one piece." My grousing fell on deaf ears.

Exactly twenty-seven minutes later we pulled up to a racetrack. "OK, what's going on?"

"It's race day!" Inga was giddy. "The F3 series is here." She stepped out of the car, and I hurriedly followed. My equilibrium couldn't handle another minute in the passenger's seat.

"So you like NASCAR?" My knowledge of racing was limited to that movie about Ricky Bobby. And the Disney cartoon about cars.

"It's not NASCAR." She rolled her eyes at my ignorance. "It's Formula 3. Open-wheel racing. It's like an entry version of your Indy Car."

"Oh," I feigned recognition.

"You have no idea what I'm talking about, do you?"

"Not a clue."

"You'll learn." Inga tossed her hair and walked toward the grandstand. "I have an eternity to teach you."

We made our way through the concessions line before settling into our seats.

"So you're, uh, a car fan?"

"Yes." Inga's delighted laughter attracted the attention of several men nearby. They eyed her appreciatively. "I love driving, and I'd love to race. But as I'm sure Ull told you, we're supposed to stay under the radar. We certainly couldn't enter a competition like this without being noticed. Obviously, we'd take the pole."

"Of course." So the prize was a pole. I'd expected something fancier.

"So I just watch. Gunnar and Ull have their rugby and I have this. Besides, now I have the chance to talk to you alone."

"Shoot." I sipped my soda.

"Kristia, you're the Seer! That's a huge deal. How are you dealing with it?"

I jumped when the cars started their engines on the track, a dozen or so claps of thunder just ten yards away. "It's fine."

"Kristia . . ."

Truthfully, I wasn't entirely sure what it all meant. "What?"

"You're the Seer."

"I know." I tried not to twitch. "It's a big to do, my mental problem's going to get a lot worse, and now I have to have some stupid bodyguard follow me around twenty-four hours a day."

"Of course you do." Inga scrunched her impeccably groomed eyebrows together. "You're the Seer."

"So?"

"What do you mean, 'so'? Has anyone explained to

you what you are? I mean, really sat you down and explained it to you?"

"I've got the general idea."

"Do you really?"

"Okay, no."

"Here's the deal. Yours was the very first prophecy the Three Sisters ever made, before Ragnarok, before the Jotun Rebellion, before any of it. They predicted someone would come with all-powerful sight—the ability to predict the future, see the past, and know everything happening in all the realms in the present. And that person would be able to protect their allies against any attack. Forever."

"And they decided this person would be a human?" These sisters must not have been the sharpest crayons in the box.

"No. The prophecy wasn't specific, but we all kind of figured they were talking about an Aesir."

"An Aesir?"

"The main gods in Asgard: Odin, Balder, Thor . . . their group." Inga shrugged.

"Got it."

"But time went on and nobody fulfilled the prophecy. We didn't exactly forget about it, but we started to wonder if they'd been wrong. It's been millennia."

"Did you ever think to look in another realm?" Though it seemed unlikely the Norns would have chosen a fire giant for a peacekeeping job.

"No. They've never given such an important prophecy to someone who wasn't an Aesir or a Vanir."

"Vanir?" I asked.

"The next rung of gods. The rest of us."

"Oh."

"Thank Odin Ull found you. You have to become a goddess to fulfill your prophecy."

"Right." I sighed. "And I get a bodyguard."

"That's what's bugging you? Not being hunted into perpetuity by every enemy of Asgard?"

Well, now that she mentioned it . . .

"I know you don't want a guard, but you're ridiculously valuable. Odin will make sure you're taken care of."

"Sure. Some stranger's going to follow me around twenty-four-seven, know everything I do and report back to management. Fantastic."

"It's a lot of change, isn't it?" Inga squeezed my hand, her soft voice somehow carrying over the thrum of the engines below.

"It's fine." I stared at the cars. "So who's it going to be?"

Inga watched the cars with me. "It was going to be Skadi."

"What?" I exploded. "Skadi, the girl Thor wanted Ull to marry—that Skadi? Shadowing everything I do?" My feathers were in a full-on fluff.

"Don't be so dramatic." Inga rolled her eyes. "I told him that wasn't going to work. I wouldn't let my best friend get stuck with a dark troll."

"You know Skadi?" I asked.

"Of course. I'm her trainer."

"Like at the gym?"

"No, silly. You know how we all have assignments back in Asgard?" Inga shifted to get a better look at the track.

"Yes."

"Gunnar's an assassin, Ull's God of Winter, and I'm a tactical advisor to the warriors. I orchestrate their fight sequences and train the warriors to execute them."

"Seriously?" Inga was a tough cookie, but I'd had no idea.

"Yes. I'd rather be a fighter, but it makes Dad too nervous. So he asked Odin to put me in a non-combat position with the warriors."

"Do you work with Skadi?" I asked.

"Ugh. Skadi's in my training group, and she is a piece of work." Inga didn't take her eyes off the track. One of the cars shifted to pass another and nearly hit the wall as it went by. Jeez.

"What do you mean?"

"Well, besides being ridiculously impressed with herself, she's madder than a fire giant in Jotunheim."

"Why?"

"Who knows?" Inga shrugged. "She's always been crazy. And she's always had a weird thing for Ull. Don't worry," she added when I bristled. "He's never been into her. Like, ever."

"Good." It was hard not to be insecure about the warrior goddess Thor wanted to marry his son.

"But because she's so uppity and crazy, and because she somehow thinks she's entitled to Ull, I told Dad she wasn't a good candidate for your bodyguard position. He thought she'd be perfect, that she could pretend to be a co-ed and go to class with you. Yeah, right. There's nothing collegiate about that mountain goat."

I giggled. "So she didn't get the job?"

"Nope. I heard she was really mad about it, too. She probably thought if she were that close to Ull, she'd win him over or something." Inga leaned over and slapped my hand away from my face. "Kristia! Don't bite your nails this close to your wedding!"

"Sorry." I twirled with the straw in my drink instead. "So who's going to be my jailer now?"

"Bodyguard. And I don't know. I wish it could be me."

"Why can't it be?" That was a great idea. Inga and I already spent loads of time together. If I had to have someone following me around, it may as well have been someone I enjoyed hanging out with.

"Too dangerous." Her hair shook around her shoulders. "Dad's convinced that every dark elf in the cosmos is going to come after you the minute your identity comes out. And he doesn't want me standing in their way. Kristia! Nails! Nobody's going to get you. Ull won't let them."

"Right." I gripped my cup to keep my hands busy. "So you're sure there was never anything between Skadi and Ull?"

"I'm sure. Honestly, Kristia, he never looked twice at anybody before he met you."

"Uh-huh."

"Seriously. After his dad died, he couldn't handle

the thought of losing anyone else."

"Well, he's never getting rid of me."

"I know." Inga leaned forward in her seat as two cars spun out. A man on the track waved a yellow flag and the racers slowed down. "And *you're* never getting rid of me. It's been an eternity of exhaustion taking care of the boys by myself. Did I tell you what Gunnar did to my new paring knife?"

She started the latest in a series of tales of Gunnar destroying her beloved kitchenware. I let my mind focus on Inga's domestic difficulties while the cars moved slowly around the wreck. I could think about my worries another day.

CHAPTER FIVE

WHEN I GOT BACK to my flat, my roommates were lying in wait.

"Where have you been?" Victoria sat in the armchair in our small living area, staring at the door like an annoyed parent. Her chic chestnut hair was fixed into a sleek bob, and she twirled her stiletto-clad foot at the ankle. Even relaxing at home, my fashion-major flatmate managed to look like she just stepped off the runway.

With a glance at the clock in the entryway, I closed the front door behind me. "It's five-thirty. We aren't supposed to leave for dinner until six. You know I'd never miss Curry Thursday."

That was a lie. I'd have given my eyeteeth to have Chow Mein Thursday, but Cardiff was disappointingly devoid of good Chinese restaurants. It was an outright sin.

"Yes, well, I've got some wedding designs to go over with you. And Emma has been waiting all afternoon to try her Hair Helper."

"Hair Helper?"

"Yes. Finally! Jeez, took you long enough. Come on, we only have thirty minutes until we have to leave." Emma flew down the hallway, her crimson hair streaming behind her. I caught a glimpse of the strange contraption in her hand as she dragged me into her bedroom. She shoved me down onto her bed and climbed up after me, pulling the elastic out of my ponytail.

"What are you doing?" I tried to crane my neck but she held my head in place with a surprisingly strong grip.

"We need to practice your wedding hair," Emma declared.

"My wedding hair?" I turned to the other side and stared at the domed object in Emma's hands. "What is that thing?"

"The Hair Helper. It's guaranteed to give you real 'oomph' at the crown. I ordered it off the late-night telly."

"Oh, Emma. You haven't been shopping off that again, have you?" Emma was a math major, and one of the brightest analytical minds I'd met at Cardiff, but she had some seriously questionable hobbies. The last time she'd ordered something from the shopping network, we enjoyed savory purees for our stews . . . . until the Dream Dome exploded, leaving tiny bits of carrots and onions all over our kitchen.

"She has, and now you get to reap the rewards." Victoria strolled into the bedroom, sketchpad in hand.

I jumped to my feet. "I really don't think—"

“Sit back down. This is happening.” Emma pushed me back into position and shoved the weird thing at my head. It looked about as useful as a screen door on a submarine, but Emma was determined. She started smoothing strands of hair over the Velcro-covered peak, sticking out her tongue as she concentrated.

“And you thought living with a fashion major was irritating.” Victoria made herself comfortable against the headboard, then smoothed her hair.

“At least that has perks,” I conceded. “No good can come of this.”

“Please,” Emma huffed. “You’ll have me to thank when you knock Ull’s socks off walking down the aisle.”

“I hope that’s not the only article of clothing she knocks off of Ull.” Victoria uncapped her pen and started to draw. “Where are you going on your honeymoon?”

“I don’t know. Ull won’t tell me.”

“Ooh, so romantic!” Emma squealed. She clapped her hands and pushed me to the mirror. “Well, with hair this fabulous, you won’t need to pack much.”

Victoria looked up from her sketchpad. “Just a baseball cap.”

“Don’t you like it?” Emma’s face fell.

I glanced in the mirror and tried not to cringe. My hair was stuck in a weird cone-shape on top of my head, with strands sticking at odd angles away from my face. Instinct told me this was supposed to be some sort of an elegant bouffant, but in reality I looked like I’d just stuck my finger in an electrical socket. I wracked my brain for something nice to say, but came up with diddly squat. There was just nothing good about this particular look.

Thankfully the chimes in my pocket did the talking for me.

"Pachelbel's Canon. Must be the lucky fiancé." Victoria snickered as I pulled out my phone.

"Seriously, Kristia? Still with the flip phone?" Emma shook her head. "I told you I'd take you to the Apple store on Saturday to—"

"Hold on a sec, Ull. I just have to do something real quick." I put my phone down and began tugging at the top of my head. When I'd emancipated my mane, I tossed the contraption to Emma. "On second thought, I think I'm going to wear my hair down for the wedding." I shrugged apologetically and patted her hand. "But thanks for thinking of me."

"But—"

"What's up, Ull?" I stepped into the hallway.

"I just wanted to make sure you got home from the racetrack safely." His deep voice sent a shiver down my spine.

"Just barely. Inga drives like a maniac."

"I know. You have not had any more visions since the one at Ýdalir?"

"Nope." I glanced at my roommates to see if they were listening, but they were staring at the Hair Helper.

"You will tell me immediately if you do." It was a command.

"I promised I would."

"You know how important this is. If you see anything suspicious, if you have any odd feelings, or a dream that you think might be—"

"Ull, I get it," I whispered. "I'll come straight to you if anything weird happens. But I have to go. It's curry night."

"You hate curries."

"I do not," I protested. "I just . . . uh . . ."

"Kristia, can't we just try one more hairstyle before we leave?" Emma pleaded. "I think I know what I did wrong."

"I have to go, Ull. Girl's night."

"Call when you get home to let me know you are safe," he ordered.

"I will."

"And Kristia? *Jeg elsker deg.*"

"I love you, too," I murmured as I closed my phone.

"So one more style? Then dinner?" Emma asked hopefully.

I shook my head.

"Let it go, Emma. She's just not ready for the Hair Helper." Victoria patted Emma's arm.

"That was just my first go at it. I still have three months to practice on her before the wedding."

Three months . . .

"That's barely enough time for me to design your going-away gown." Victoria patted the bed.

"You're going to design a dress for me?" My eyes felt moist. "That is so incredibly kind."

"Of course I am. It's not every day one's roommate makes an honest man of the sexiest bloke on campus.

What do you think of my sketches?" Victoria held up her notebook. I sat down and took the pad from her hands. When I opened the cover, I bit back a smile.

"This is gorgeous, Victoria." It was. A Grecian-style sheath with wide straps, an empire waist, and an exaggerated fitted bodice that tapered all the way to the ankle. "But I'm afraid it's more you than me. I'd never be able to walk in it. And I'm not entirely sure my tush would fit in . . . there." I gestured.

"Your bum would look amazing in it. What about this one? Emma inspired it." Victoria flipped the page and I giggled.

"That is definitely you, Em."

"It is, isn't it? Sweetheart neck, fit-and-flare waist, a double petticoated miniskirt. The oversized flower appliqués would be either organza or chiffon. I want it to have an ethereal feel—like wearing a cloud." Victoria pointed with her pencil.

"It's spectacular," I agreed.

"You could wear it with one of those tiaras we saw last week! Or a feathered fascinator—ooh, a feathered fascinator." Emma's eyes glazed over as she went to a fashion-inspired happy place.

"And then there's this one." Victoria turned the page again. "I think this would suit you best."

I tore my eyes away from the now-bouncing Emma and stared at the page. My hand flew to my neck—Victoria's design took my breath away. The sleeveless dress had a fitted bodice that would accentuate my chest. The skirt skimmed the hips tightly enough to showcase my . . . assets . . . before flaring in a delicate bell shape. It ended a few inches above the knee. It was just modest enough that Mormor would have approved, but still sexy enough to wow a Norse god. The dress had an intricate lace design that looked like a series of paisley swirls and delicate flowers, and it appeared to have some kind of beading sewn throughout—Victoria had drawn little lines designating sparkles.

"Wow." I exhaled.

"You haven't seen the best part." Victoria turned the page again, revealing another sketch. "Check out that back."

"Holy mother." Emma sidled up next to us. "It drops almost to your bum. That backline is sexy as sin. Ull won't be able to keep his hands off you."

"That was the plan." Victoria confirmed.

"Um . . ." My fingers covered my eyes. The idea of wearing a near-backless dress had me flustered. But the idea of Ull and his hands . . . "Yes. Please. Make that one." *Make it right now.*

"You like it?" Victoria shot me a sly glance.

"I love it," I confirmed.

"But more importantly, Ull is going to flip." Emma tossed her hair. "Has he ever seen you in anything that sexy?"

"Emma," Victoria said. "Please."

"My clothes are sexy," I defended myself.

"Sure. If you call the occasionally exposed collarbone or, *gasp*, a bare wrist sexy," Emma heckled.

Victoria narrowed her eyes. "She does have a point." She buried her head in her sketchpad, scribbling furiously.

"It's not like we had any reason to wear backless gowns in Nehalem," I pointed out. "It was cold, like, three hundred days a year."

"How do you explain the other sixty-five days?" Emma nudged me with her shoulder.

"Okay, ladies. What if we did something like this for a honeymoon dress?" Victoria held up the paper. "In teal, or maybe white."

"Oh my God, V. It's perfect! Can you make me one in green?" Emma clapped her hands.

"You just came up with that?" I touched the paper with one finger.

"The strapless bit might be a little uncomfortable for you, but we'll tuck it here and here," Victoria pointed with her pencil, "and I'll build in padded cups so you don't have to worry about fidgeting with a bra. The ruching will accentuate your tiny waist, and the A-line will give Ull easy access in the event he decides to—"

"It's gorgeous," I interrupted, blushing fiercely. "Love the ribbon at the hips."

"That is a nice touch, don't you think?" Victoria admired her work. "We could even add some pockets. Fun it up."

"You're really going to make me two dresses?" I touched the notebook with one hand.

"I'm planning to make you an entire honeymoon wardrobe. No offense, Kristia, but I don't trust you to shop for yourself for *that* particular occasion."

Now that she mentioned it, some guidance would

be nice.

"Yay!" Emma clapped her hands. "What about something like this for one of the dresses?" She grabbed the pencil out of Victoria's hands and started drawing. When she finished, Victoria eyed the paper critically.

"Again with the eyelets? Emma, we *discussed* this. Leave the design to me. You just worry about Kristia's wedding hair." Victoria smiled angelically as Emma grabbed the Hair Helper off the nightstand.

"Oh, goody. Because I think I know what happened before, and it's an easy fix. All we have to do is tease the crown and maybe add some of that glittery hairspray . . ."

Heaven help us all.

❄ ❄ ❄ ❄

"Olaug! To what do I owe the honor?" I opened the door of my flat with a wide smile. Olaug stood on the other side, an overflowing grocery bag in her arms.

"I was just passing through, and I thought I'd pop in on my soon-to-be-granddaughter. And her roommates—are they home?"

"No. They've got classes this afternoon." Holding the door open with my hip, I reached for her bag. "Let me take that for you, it looks heavy. Come in. I'm so happy you're here."

Olaug patted my arm as she walked into our tiny entry. While I carried the bag to the kitchen, she took off her coat and appraised our living space. Couch facing the open kitchen, tartan throw artfully arranged across the reading chair, and thanks to a bout of pre-honeymoon jitters, a freshly swept and mopped floor. Everything was spic and span.

"What a lovely home, Kristia," Olaug praised.

"Thank you." Heat crept across my cheeks as I made my way back to the foyer. "Let me take your coat."

With the coat tucked away in the closet, I followed Olaug toward the kitchen. "Can I get you anything? Tea, or a sandwich, or maybe some cookies?"

"Actually my dear, I brought you something. Oh good, you do have a stand mixer. Makes it so much easier." Olaug made herself at home in my kitchen, unpacking the grocery bag and rooting through drawers until she pulled out our mixing bowls. "This will do nicely."

"What are we making?" My smile was genuine. It had been so long since I'd cooked with Mormor. Continuing the tradition with Olaug was an unexpected perk of becoming a Myhr.

"There's no way I can allow you to marry my grandson without teaching you to make his favorite waffles." Olaug rooted around my kitchen until she found the aprons. She handed one to me and tied the other around her waist. "Suit up, Kristia. We have much to cover."

"You're teaching me to make your waffles? Your Norsk Waffles? The recipe Inga's been trying to get out of you forever?"

"The very one."

"Wow." I exhaled. "This is huge."

"You are family now. I always knew I would share

my recipe with Ull's bride, I just didn't know I'd have to wait this long to meet her."

When the apron was tied tightly around my back, I pulled out a fresh hand towel. "Is this a goddess lesson day, too? I feel like we've barely scratched the surface, and there's not a lot of time left."

"I feel the same way." Olaug plugged in the mixer. "Do you have time to go over some things? If not, we can just make a quick batch of waffles and I will get out of your hair."

"No! Stay, please. My afternoon is free as a bee."

"Excellent. Then please hand me three eggs."

"Hold on. I won't remember all of this." I ran to my bedroom and returned with a notebook and a pen. "Okay. Go."

Olaug chuckled. "You do realize much about being of Asgard will be instinctual, don't you? The relationships, the extrasensory enhancements, they are just going to come to you as you go along. They are not things that can be taught."

"Maybe. But I also know an extra half-teaspoon of vanilla can completely wreck a batch of chocolate chip cookies. And I'm not taking any chances with Ull's waffles."

"Fair enough." Olaug smiled. "Whip the eggs thoroughly." My pen flew across the paper as I took verbatim dictation. "Make sure the butter is completely melted, and do *not* overuse the cardamom. You will want to, but the savory should never overpower the sweet."

"How much do I use?"

"Some."

"I'm going to need something more specific than that." Compulsion wasn't a hat one could just take off.

"I've never measured it. I just use some."

I dug through a drawer until I came up with measuring spoons. "How about this. I'll hold these over the bowl so I can measure what 'some' means and write it down."

Olaug smiled. "If you wish." She added the remaining ingredients and patted my hand. "The sugar comes next. Whip it into the eggs until the mixture is slightly stiff."

She continued, adding her personal touches to each ingredient as she cooked. Finally, the batter was ready.

"Oops. Should have plugged my waffle iron in sooner. Sorry!" I moved to pull my iron from the cupboard, but Olaug put a hand to my arm.

"Norsk waffles have their own kind of iron." She pulled a heart shaped waffle maker from the bottom of the grocery bag. It heated quickly, and in no time we sat at the kitchen table with two fresh cups of Earl Grey and a batch of homemade waffles.

"These are amazing." Flavor danced around the corners of my mouth as I took another bite. "Even better than the ones at the church."

"I have had a veritable eternity to perfect them," Olaug pointed out. "And speaking of eternity, let's talk about your new life. When you and Ull promise 'till death do us part,' it's going to mean a whole lot longer than you grew up thinking it would."

"I know. I can't wait."

"Look at you." Olaug reached across the table to pat my hand. "Your smile could be seen from the heavens. I've only ever seen one bigger. Ull just lights up when you are around. It is such a blessing to see you two together."

Heat tickled the back of my neck. "You love him so much."

"Of course." Olaug pulled her hand away to spread jam on a waffle. "I used to take care of him while his mother was away. Did he ever tell you about it?"

"Ull doesn't talk about his childhood."

"I know." Olaug's voice was soft. "It was an unhappy time for him. After his father passed and Sif married Thor, she was away for months at a time in battle. In Asgard, when you marry you assume your husband's position, and as you will become Goddess to Ull's God of Winter title, Sif became Thor's battle goddess. She followed him off to fight, and left her little boy in my care."

"But didn't she want to be with Ull all the time? Especially after everything he'd been through?" If I were lucky enough to have a family, I wouldn't leave them for anything. I'd be there for my babies' first steps, first words, first everything. There would be no way I'd leave them for months at a time. Ever.

"It didn't matter what she wanted." Olaug watched me carefully. "This is the way things are done in Asgard. The Aesir have a duty to the realm that supersedes duty to self."

"Are you saying that if Ull and I get to have

children, I won't be allowed to be with them?" My heart squeezed.

"I am saying that unless *someone* shakes things up, Asgard will continue to operate the same as it has done for millennia. And in my humble opinion, that would be a true travesty. I like *endre*." Olaug lifted her waffle.

"*Endre*?" I repeated.

"It means change," Olaug explained. "Someone has to be the one to bring it to Asgard. Don't you agree it's time?"

Oh.

I gave a tiny nod as Olaug took a bite. When she'd finished chewing, she wiped the corner of her mouth with a napkin. "Now as Goddess of Winter, you and Ull actually have a fairly non-confrontational assignment. Not to say it is not difficult, but it is a non-combat position, which is rare among the Aesir. Since Odin has always given Ull discretion in performing his duties, I would imagine you would be able to stay together the majority of the time. There will be some travel as weather anomalies pop up in the realms, but for the most part you will be able to choose a base and work out of it. Together."

"That's good." It would have been scary to think about navigating immortality all by my lonesome.

"Ull does a significant amount of research for his post. Satellites move around all nine realms, transmitting data to whichever base he is working out of. Ull analyzes the patterns, looks for trends, and performs necessary adjustments."

"How does he do that, exactly?" *And more importantly, how was I supposed to do it with him?*

"He hasn't shown you? He is able to manipulate the climate with his hands."

"Excuse me?" There was no way she was being serious.

"Kristia, he is God of Winter. He draws on his Odin-given gift and generates weather patterns through his hands. He sends them to the necessary coordinates through the teleportation system he developed with Heimdall. If the situation is truly extreme, he visits the climate personally and performs necessary adjustments." Olaug tilted her head. "What did you think he did at work?"

"I—I don't know." My fingers tore apart the heart-shaped waffle. "I guess I hadn't really thought about *how* he controlled the weather. Seriously? With his hands? He just . . ." I waved my hand across the table and wiggled my fingers, miming falling snow. "Poof?"

"It's a little more complicated, but yes. Poof." Olaug's eyes crinkled.

"And I'll be able to . . . *poof*, too?"

"You will. At your transformation, the power will be ingrained and Ull will be able to show you how to channel it. Along with your other powers."

"My other powers?" The waffle fell onto my plate. "What else will I get to do? Am I going to get the speedy thing Inga has?"

"Of course. Speed of movement, enhanced sight, increased strength, and enhanced physical sensitivity are just some of the changes you'll see after your transformation."

"Enhanced physical sensitivity?" I squeaked.

"Yes. It's innate in all goddesses, but it will be especially strong in you because of your title. You'll be able to feel a storm coming just by the way the moisture in your skin adjusts. If a dry season is approaching, you will know it by the way your hair and nails react to the air. Even the slightest atmospheric shift will resonate within you. Your nerve endings are going to heighten in ways most goddesses won't ever experience. It will help you tremendously in your work."

So I was going to marry Ull, turn into a goddess, and traipse off on my honeymoon with heightened sensitivity? Did anyone else see this as a ginormous recipe for disaster?

"Awesome."

"Are you frightened, Kristia?"

Was I frightened? The fate of the cosmos rested on my being able to use my visions for the greater good, but I had no idea how to properly channel them. If I didn't get a grip on my mental tic soon, things were going to end very badly for everyone I loved.

Frightened didn't even begin to cover what I was.

A shudder danced along the length of my spine. I hated the feeling of being so grossly underprepared. But as much as I wanted to ask Olaug to help me practice using my visions *right now*, I knew she'd give me the official Asgardian party line—*It's too soon. It's too dangerous. Wait until after you're changed.* I took a breath and relegated my panic into the corner of my brain. My anxieties could be dealt with later.

"I'm a little scared," I admitted. "Doesn't mean I don't want to go through with this though. I would do anything to spend a thousand lifetimes with Ull."

"I know you would." Olaug leaned back in her chair. "It is what made me love you every bit as much as he does. Ull never let himself wish for a family. I was afraid he was broken. But you have given me faith. That he sees a future for himself, after all of this time . . . it is a miracle."

"I'll take care of him, Olaug. I promise."

She hugged me tightly. "You will take care of each other."

❄ ❄ ❄ ❄

That night, I paced my room. The Asgardians told me I wouldn't be able to fully control my visions until I'd been transformed, but Olaug's comment had really gotten to me. I *was* frightened. Mormor hadn't raised me to sit helplessly on the sidelines, and I didn't like doing it one bit. I was sick of waiting to do something to help my soon-to-be family. Ull had waited lifetimes to find me, and here I was sitting on my mental tic like it was an unwanted birthday present. I didn't want to wait any more. It was time to test-run my gift.

Elsker wasn't scheduled to give me my first formal training session for another week, but we'd talked a little on the phone. From the *very* little she'd told me, I gathered I was supposed to get to a calm space in my head, breathe deeply, and ground myself to the earth. Then I could project a part of myself wherever I wanted to go. Apparently once I was changed, some special Asgardian power would kick in and make this all easier, but so long as I was human it was nearly impossible. Pish. Mormor used to claim I was so stubborn I'd argue with a lamppost. If there hadn't been so much truth to those words, I'd have admitted she was right.

I knew Ull and Elsker were just trying to protect me. They were so nervous about all of this. And while I knew what I was doing was risky—I hadn't forgotten Ull's warning about being kidnapped and losing all my powers, or the whole burning pajamas debacle—the way I saw it, I'd had these visions my whole life without any training anyway. What was the worst that could happen?

I closed my eyes and focused on the backs of my eyelids. Then I pictured a rope pulling me down to the floor. There. That should be grounding enough. Now, to the traveling. I didn't have anything I really needed to see, and I was smart enough not to go looking for Asgard's enemies on my first go-round. So I pictured the living room. It was only forty feet away. An image of the couch came to mind and I bit my cheek, focusing on the throw pillows.

"Come on, alleged Asgardian power." I clutched my grandmother's necklace for luck. "Show me how this works." I opened one eye; I hadn't moved. And neither had my spirit, or whatever it was that Ull failed to explain back at Ýdalir. I squeezed my eyes shut and pictured the couch again, this time imagining my body floating toward it. I peeked from one lowered eyelid—still nothing.

I closed my eyes a third time and squeezed the necklace so hard the tiny hammer stabbed my hand. Suddenly I did feel something, but it wasn't what I'd been going for. Needles pierced my skull from all sides and the backs of my eyeballs felt like they were on fire. My head throbbed and I grabbed at my temples. My chest rose and fell with no control on my part, and my body shook violently.

In all my nightmares, I'd never once given in to the pain. But with one final shake, I was consumed by the darkness.

I never even saw it coming.

CHAPTER SIX

"KRISTIA!" EMMA'S SHRIEK BROUGHT me back from the darkness. Cold hands cupped my cheeks while something damp dabbed at my forehead. Was it a washrag? My eyes burned too much to open.

"Where am I?" My voice sounded shaky.

"In the living room. My God, Kristia, what happened? You've been convulsing for like, two minutes! You're covered in sweat. We need to get you to the hospital."

"In the living room . . ." I was in the living room. So I had done it then? But I wasn't supposed to have actually moved—I'd only meant to travel in my mind. And I hadn't seen mental pictures of the living room, only flashes of light as I'd been overcome with pain. "How did I get here?"

"I have no idea! We just heard a thud and came running."

"Hospital, Kristia. Now." Victoria was here too; both girls were in their pajamas. They must have jumped out of bed to help me.

"No, no thank you." I sat up slowly. The pain that wracked my body ebbed just a tad. "I'm okay, really."

"You are not."

"Yes, I swear. I just need to lie down."

Skeptically, Victoria helped me onto the couch while Emma ran for a glass of water. They sat with me until I convinced them I really was fine, which took two full episodes of *Sports Wives*. When the last episode ended, I let them walk me to my room.

"Are you sure you are all right? Have you ever had a seizure before?"

"I swear, Emma. I'm fine. Really. I'll yell if I need anything."

"You can't yell if you're having a seizure," Victoria pointed out.

"I just . . . need to sleep. Really," I added when Victoria gave me a pointed stare.

"All right. But if you want to tuck in with one of us just to be safe, you should probably head to my room. Emma snores."

"I do not!" Emma squealed.

"You sure you will be all right, Kristia?" Victoria crossed her arms.

"I swear. I'm okay. Go to bed, really."

"We're right down the hall if you need anything." Emma patted my legs and followed Victoria across the hall. I could hear their concerned whispers as they walked.

When they'd finally gone back to their rooms and all the lights were off, I grabbed my mobile from the nightstand dialed.

Olaug picked up on the third ring.

"I kind of did something." My tone was steeped in guilt. Olaug listened to my confession in silence.

"Elsker and I told you not to try this on your own. You do not have the abilities to use this gift yet."

"Clearly," I grumbled.

"You are not supposed to physically travel. Can you imagine what would happen if you sent your *body* to the frost giants? Or the dark elves? Do you have any idea what they would do to you?" I knew Olaug was very upset with me.

"I'm so sorry, Olaug. I should never have done this."

"You are right, you never should have done this. Thank Odin you only tried to see your living room. And thank Odin your friends were home. You could have been seriously hurt. Wait." She stopped her tirade. "How did you manage to move?"

"I don't know. I just did. I'm sorry, Olaug, I promise I won't try it again until I've been changed." I felt awful—Olaug had put a lot of effort into keeping me safe and getting me into Asgard. Here I was, throwing it away like yesterday's leftovers because I couldn't wait just a few more weeks.

"You had better not try this again, young lady. But how did you move? You are not a goddess yet; Asgard's magic should not have worked on you."

"Seriously, Olaug, I have no idea. I was picturing the living room and holding my necklace and—"

"Your necklace." She made the connection I hadn't. "It is elfin made." An image of Elfie flashed in my mind, but I pushed it out.

"So? Wait, does this have anything to do with the Seer thing? Because honestly, the necklace has been really helpful with the whole Elf Man situation."

"Kristia," Olaug admonished. "Everything you do for the rest of your existence will have to do with you being the Seer. You do realize this?"

"I'm starting to."

Her voice softened. "It is a tremendous honor to have been chosen, but it must also feel like a great burden. Especially as you are not from our world."

"About that." I'd been wondering. "How did a human end up being the one these Sisters prophesied to have this . . ." This what? Curse? Extreme inconvenience? Living nightmare? ". . . this power?"

"I do not know." Olaug sighed. "It does not make sense that they would go outside the Aesir and Vanir. And Elsker cannot tell us why. The Sisters never explain their prophecies, even to their lesser Norns."

Of course. I was gifted with a power Odin literally gave his eye for, and nobody seemed to know how I got so lucky.

"Is Odin upset they chose me instead of a real god? Like him?"

"He does not understand their choice, but he does not question it. He knows we each have our role to fill, and it was not his destiny to wield this power."

So the ruler of Asgard was Zen. Even so, I'd have wagered good money he wished he'd asked the Norns about his fate before he handed over his eyeball.

"What does this all have to do with my necklace?"

No point beating a dead fish. I moved back to the original question.

"Well, elfin-made objects bear elfin magic."

"So it's elf magic that's making my necklace work? I thought it was Mjölnir?"

"It is both. As The Seer, you can channel Mjölnir's magic through your necklace, but as a human, elfin magic can channel through you. It would not happen to a god; Asgardians are too powerful for that kind of magic. But because you are still human . . ." She sighed. "Kristia, please promise me you will not try this again until you have been changed and Elsker can properly train you. If you accidentally channeled the wrong kind of magic when you were trying to . . ." I could almost see her shaking her head on the other end of the phone. "Not to mention you do not know how to control your own energy. You have no idea how dangerous this could have been."

"I won't do it again. I'm sorry, really. I promise I'll listen to you the next time you tell me not to do something."

"You had better. Ull will never forgive me if I let anything happen to you."

"I know."

"And Kristia," Olaug continued, "I'm afraid I cannot let Elsker instruct you until after you are changed. If the elfin magic affected you this strongly, then it is too risky to let it access your human form. Elsker can work with you as soon as you are back from your honeymoon. *After* you are immortal."

"Aw." I sighed, but I didn't argue. I'd made a pretty

bad judgment call tonight. Best to put my faith in the gods.

"I understand. And I won't do anything until after I'm changed. I swear." It was only a few more weeks, after all. I could control myself until then . . . couldn't I?

❄ ❄ ❄ ❄

It was not shaping up to be my night. I spent an hour counting the leaves on the tree outside my window before I passed out, and once I finally did, I was plagued with what I could only assume was a bridezilla-level wedding nightmare. I'd never even seen the girl Thor had chosen for Ull, so I had no idea if the one in my nightmare looked anything like the real Skadi. And since Ull had been more than clear that he'd never considered marrying her, I had no reason to be insecure, but as I tossed and turned, I dreamed about the goddess Ull's father thought would be his perfect match.

"You can't be serious, Njord. You're dumping me?" An almost-pretty brunette sat on a granite bench. The long corridor was bordered with beveled columns, opening onto the lake surrounding the palace. It was clear to even my un-indoctrinated brain that we were somewhere inside an Asgardian castle.

"Try not to think of it like that, Skadi," Njord pleaded with her. He was a handsome man with light eyes—a slighter, less intimidating version of Ull. "You know as well as I do you're in love with someone else."

"So?" Skadi swiped at her tears. "I'm with you, aren't I?"

Njord sat beside her. "I can't spend my life with

someone who doesn't love me."

"I love you. Just not the way you want me to." Skadi's chocolate hair rippled around her shoulders as she let out a sigh. "I'm not like the rest of you."

Njord rested a hand on Skadi's knee. "I know you feel that way. But you're a fighter. You could be happy if you let yourself."

"Yeah, right."

Njord shook his head. "You're stronger than that. You're an Asgardian."

"Maybe I'm cut from a different cloth than the rest of you."

"Maybe you are." Njord stood and looked down at her.

"Don't do that. I don't need your pity." Skadi rose, and for the first time I saw that she was tall—very tall. She'd have towered over me, and she stood eye to eye with Njord. Her sleeveless dress revealed thick, muscular arms and though she moved with typical Asgardian grace, she wasn't what anyone would call delicate.

"I don't pity you. I just wish you could see what I see in you."

"Right. Because obviously you see just enough to dump me."

"I told you, it's not—"

"I don't need you. Ull loves me more than you ever did. The prophecy just confused him."

"Skadi." Njord touched her shoulder and she jerked away. "Ragnarok is not the reason Ull turned you down."

"Yes. It is." Skadi spoke through clenched teeth. "Now that we're older he can appreciate what I have to offer."

"Oh, Skadi." Njord stepped in to touch her, but Skadi slapped his hand away. "You haven't heard."

"Haven't heard what?"

"Ull is getting married. To a mortal."

Skadi was silent for a full ten seconds before the corridor was filled with animalistic shrieking.

"Ull fell in love with a human during one of his trips to Midgard. She knows what he is and she's willing to stand with him at Ragnarok. They're getting married this summer and Odin's going to make her a goddess. Thor even signed off on it."

"Thor likes me," Skadi practically spat the words.

"Apparently the human won him over."

"She's going to be a goddess? Can that even happen?"

"I guess." Njord crossed his arms over his chest. "Things are changing here. Ragnarok is coming. Odin couldn't lose Ull so close to the final battle. Letting the mortal in was the only way to keep him."

"The only way." Skadi balled the fabric of her dress in sizeable hands. "What about me? He can marry me. We can fight together."

"You can still fight together," Njord pointed out. "We're going to need every warrior we have. You know that."

"I'm supposed to fight for a realm that's letting humans in?"

"Not humans," Njord corrected her. "One human.

The woman Ull loves."

"Ull doesn't know love." Skadi paced the hallway.

Njord watched as she stalked the corridor like a caged lion. "Maybe the human showed him that life doesn't have to be miserable. There can be joy, even if the Norns did hand you a tough deck."

"If you're referring to my father, don't." Skadi stalked back down the hall. "That was years ago."

"You're obviously still hurting."

"The only thing hurting me right now is getting dumped by a complete loser. I'm twice the warrior you'll ever be." She tossed her hair over her shoulder and stared the pale man down.

"You win, Skadi." Njord held his hands up in surrender and slowly backed down the hall. The lion was about to pounce.

"You're right, I do," Skadi screamed as Njord turned on his heel and walked away. "And don't you ever forget it!" She stared at the blond god's back as he turned the corner. When he was out of sight she dropped onto the granite bench and pulled her knees to her chest. She rocked herself back and forth. "Ull does love me. We're going to be happy. Forever."

I pulled myself out of the dream as fast as I could. I didn't think it was a vision—with the exception of Elf Man's visits, my visions were consistently mundane and rarely about anything of importance. I also knew I wasn't suffering from insecurity. I'd won the bachelor god's heart and even sold Thor on changing me. But none of that mattered. I didn't want to linger in this twisted dream any longer than I already had. This was obviously the byproduct of some bizarre pre-honeymoon jitters. Or maybe I was just nervous about fitting into Asgard. Either way, I wasn't going to get back to sleep. Since the night was pretty much a wash, I grabbed my blanket and headed to the couch. I flicked through the channels until I came to Emma's favorite guilty pleasure: *Late Night Telly Shoppe*. I let the models displaying their as-seen-on-TV products numb my mind, and by some miracle I eventually drifted off.

❄❄❄❄

"Where are we going?" Ull and I had left Cardiff two hours ago, right after we finished our classes for the week. The past month had been fairly uneventful, and I hadn't felt so free in . . . ever. I was nearly done with school.

"I told you, we are taking an early honeymoon." Ull kept his eyes on the road but his smirk taunted me.

"How much longer until we get there?" Traffic on the busy street was moving slower than a Sunday afternoon.

"We will get there when we get there." He knew full well he was driving me nuts.

"Ull! Are you always going to be so cryptic?"

"Are you always going to try to ruin my surprises?"

"Point made."

"And besides . . ." Ull broke from the trail of cars and turned down a street lined with Kensington row houses. Their red-brick facades were offset with shiny white pillars and big windows. ". . . we are here."

He drove around the block, pulling into an alley where the garages were hidden. He parked in one and crossed to help me out of the Range Rover. I waited until he came around, forever cognizant of that first time I'd wacked him with my door. Oops.

"Are you going to tell me what this place is?"

Ull grabbed my hand and led me into the house, closing the garage door behind him.

"If I must," he teased. We made our way up one flight of stairs then another, each floor housing sleek, modern furniture that looked like it belonged in a showroom. The space was open and airy.

One more flight and we reached the third story. It was completely different than the other two—it reminded me of Ýdalir. Modern country furnishings dominated the space, from the overstuffed couch covered in plush throws to the dark wood of the table and chairs in the dining area and the charming lamps in the kitchen. This was more like it. Despite my choice of man, the Scandinavian furnishings that dominated the first two floors would never be my style. The much homier top floor opened onto a generous stone deck overlooking a park, bordered by a wrought iron fence.

"Seriously Ull, where are we? Did you rent this place for the weekend?"

"This is our city home."

"Our city home?" Ull had never mentioned this.

"Yes, sweetheart. I keep a residence in London—it is terribly convenient. And since we will be married soon it is yours now, too."

"We have a city home?" This was wild. I walked to

the French doors that led to the deck and touched the rich fabric of the curtains. "Is that Kensington Palace?" The structure was just a block away.

"It is. I love hearing the children in the park."

I looked again. It was springtime, and the park was covered in pale yellow daffodils. It was beautiful.

"Geez, Ull." My thoughts danced between awe and accusation. "Why didn't you ever mention this before?"

"It never came up."

He owned so many houses he could forget to mention them? The guy quite literally had it all. I walked over to the couch and curled up in its corner, picking at the wrists of my sweater.

"Sweetheart, what is wrong? Why are you sad?"

"Because it's all too much." I focused on pulling the little balls of lint at my wrists. "You have everything."

"Everything I have is yours."

"But what if I'm not any good at this?"

"At what?" Ull sat beside me.

"At any of this." I gestured around the room feebly. "At being like you. Fitting into your life. What if I end up disappointing you?"

"You could never disappoint me."

"Fine. Even if I'm okay at being a goddess, which is a huge *if*, what if I'm not any good at being a wife? I'm a decent cook, my grandmother made sure of that, but I can't iron at all. Never learned how."

"Darling." Amusement upturned a corner of Ull's mouth. He thought I was ridiculous.

"Don't laugh at me!"

"I'm not laughing at you."

I wrapped my arms around my knees, and stared at the houndstooth throw folded neatly in a basket. "Yes you are."

"My love, do you really think I would leave you because you cannot iron? While it is a terrible travesty," Ull eyed me gravely and I swatted at him, "you must realize I have been living on my own for a long time. I can iron."

"Oh." *I forgot about that.* "That's right."

Ull pulled at my arms until I released my grip on my legs. He drew them across his lap. "Kristia, you will make a fine wife. Just keep being yourself."

Laughter rang through the open French doors, and I glanced at the green expanse of Kensington Park before responding. "Myself spent eighteen years in a one-light town. I'm not feeling so great about being able to keep up with the gods."

"Are you anxious, sweetheart?" Ull rested an arm lightly on the back of the couch.

Anxious. I could practically hear the sirens of the understatement police.

"Sweetheart?"

"A little," I admitted.

"Talk to me." It was an order, and I picked at my sweater again before I met Ull's eyes.

"What about Skadi?" It was more morbid curiosity than insecurity that made me bring up the other woman. I was reasonably sure my nightmare had been more dream than vision, but it was hard to shake the image of the enraged goddess set on stealing my man.

"What about her?" Ull stroked my hair.

"Are you sure you wouldn't be happier with someone like her—someone who's more like you?"

"Kristia, please. Skadi could never make me happy. You make me happy. Period. I really do not wish to talk about Skadi again."

"But what if she wanted to be with you?"

"What if she did?" For the first time, Ull betrayed a hint of impatience. "Do you really think it would change the way I feel about you?"

"I don't know." I stared at my lap. "Maybe."

"Kristia Tostenson," Ull raised my chin with a firm finger, "there is not now, has never been, and will never be anything between Skadi and I. Am I clear?"

I nodded. Relief flooded my insides.

"What about my friends?" I moved on quickly, knowing I'd exhausted his patience on the Skadi issue. "Once I'm changed, will I see them again? I mean I know I can't tell them what I become, but will I get to visit Ardis? She's been my best friend all my life. What happens to us?"

"Oh, darling. I thought Olaug had talked about this with you. I should have realized." I shivered as he touched my cheek. "Of course you will see your friends. We will visit them whenever we can. I know how important they are to you. I could never keep you from them."

"But aren't we going to have to move to Asgard?"

"I hope not. Odin has been most generous in letting me telecommute, so to speak. So long as we have adequate security for you, and so long as the threat of Ragnarok is at least somewhat distant, I imagine he will continue to allow us to work from Ýdalir with Olaug. Unless you want to move to Asgard?"

I shook my head. "I like our life here."

Ull smiled. "I do, too. Any more questions?"

"Only about a hundred. But I think that covers it for now."

"Are you sure?"

"Yes." I rested my palms on the cushions of the couch, and leaned in so our faces were nearly touching. "I'm sure." I brought my lips to his.

He caught on immediately, pulling me to him with such force it left any sense of my propriety behind. I grabbed at the thick muscles of his arms. My mood was clear. Ull seemed only too happy to acquiesce, pulling me onto his lap so suddenly my breath caught in my throat. He wrapped his fingers around my waist, holding me firmly against him. My stomach felt warm, and my limbs started to tingle. I ran my hands up his biceps and across his chest, feeling the hard muscles beneath. Ull moaned, the low sound vibrating beneath my hand. As I trailed my fingers toward his abs, Ull grabbed my wrist.

"Much as I want to do this sweetheart, we need to go."

"Where?" I panted.

Holding me in one arm he pulled two tickets out of the air with his free hand. "I believe your favorite play is in town."

"What did you just do?"

"*Much Ado About Nothing*. Your favorite, *ja*? I got us two tickets."

"No, I mean . . . did you just pull them out of the air?"

"Oh, right. I never explained the whole conjuring deal, did I? It is nothing big, just . . . one of the unusual things about me is that I have . . . extra powers. I can elicit and eradicate objects, control elements, that sort of thing. Only a handful of the gods have the ability. It is rather convenient." He shrugged like it was nothing. "I ordered these when we decided to come to London; they have been in the car. I was just too lazy to go downstairs to get them."

"So you're a magician?" Would the surprises never end?

"I have some additional abilities, yes. I do not use them often; I try not to get lazy. Though of course it is helpful in battle." He was thoughtful. "Does this worry you?"

"Not nearly as much as it probably should." My instincts told me even stranger experiences awaited me as Mrs. Ull Myhr.

Ull wrapped both arms around me and stood. He set me on my feet, then held out his hand. "Shall we go to the theatre?"

I'd never needed to take my mind off of the real world so much in my life. "Absolutely."

CHAPTER SEVEN

ULL AND GUNNAR FINISHED packing to leave on their bachelor trip when we got back to Cardiff. It would be short—just two days of fishing on a lake near the Cotswolds. When they returned, we'd have a week to cram for finals, then exams, graduation, and our wedding. It seemed like an eternity had passed since I'd first met Ull when I was visiting the British Museum. I could hardly believe how much had happened since then.

"You realize, Mr. Myhr," I folded his favorite sweater and placed it next to his waders in the suitcase on his bed, "you weren't exactly the easiest guy to get to know."

"You had your work cut out for you winning me over, *ja*?"

"Please." I glanced around the bedroom of his Cardiff flat. It was considerably smaller than the master in his London home—correction, *our* London home—but it was still distinctly Ull. Simple furnishings, a framed rugby poster . . . and a closet full of impeccably-tailored cashmere. "If I remember correctly, it was you who besieged my flat with flowers for a week before I'd even talk to you again. Good thing Emma was on her hayfever medication."

"It worked out for me in the end." Ull planted a chaste kiss on my forehead.

"This is strange." I folded a pair of jeans and put them on top of the sweater.

"My pants?"

"No. Helping you pack for your bachelor party."

"I would hardly call it a bachelor party. Bachelor parties are sordid and undignified. Gunnar and I are going fishing. A gentleman's pastime."

"Yes, heaven forbid you be undignified."

Ull raised one eyebrow. "Are you calling me stodgy?"

"If the shoe fits . . ."

Ull set aside the tackle box he was organizing and took two steps toward me. "Take it back."

"I cannot tell a lie." I made the scout's sign I'd perfected as a girl. "You're kind of stodgy."

"That is it." He pounced so quickly I barely saw him move. Before I registered anything he was next to me, pinning me to his bed. My arms were over my head and I was nose to nose with a flushed Norse god. "Take it back. Sweetheart." One corner of his mouth turned up.

"Never." My breath came in shallow gasps, drawing in the smell of soap and pine. Nobody could be expected to focus like this.

"Take. It. Back." He grazed his nose along my jaw.

"No," I whimpered.

"Then I am going to have to do this." He kissed me. Hard. He kept my hands in a firm grip with one hand and trailed two fingers down my arm and along my ribcage, before moving to caress my stomach.

I giggled. "Ull."

"Kristia." He gave me a lazy grin.

Just then his phone rang.

"Ignore it," I pleaded.

"I wish," Ull whispered before sitting up. "*Ja*?"

He kept one hand on my stomach, drawing small circles. My insides started to burn.

"Elsker. *Hvordan har du det*?" He held up one finger with an apologetic smile.

"Hi, Elsker." I sat up grudgingly and leaned over Ull's shoulder.

"*Ja*, Kristia says *hei hei*. What is going on?" His jaw tensed and he was quiet for a long time.

"What's she saying?" I whispered, but Ull's eyes were set.

"Uh-huh. Uh-huh." He frowned. "I see."

"What is it?"

"No, I understand. *Tusen takk*, Elsker." Ull ended the call.

"What's wrong?"

"Nothing, darling." He stroked my cheek with one finger.

"Bull-hooey. What's wrong? Is it Ragnarok?"

"No. She just wanted to make sure I was taking extra good care of you." He lifted my hair and kissed me behind my ear. He was obviously trying to distract me, and it worked.

"Mmm. A little to the left." I craned my neck. If I wasn't going to get any answers I might as well enjoy myself.

"Here?" He kissed me softly.

"A little lower."

"Here?" He nipped at my jaw.

I shivered. "That's nice."

"How about here?" He kissed the hollow of my neck and my eyes rolled back in my head.

"Absolutely perfect."

Thirty minutes later, Gunnar and Ull left for their fishing trip. I'd brought my overnight bag so Inga and I could relax in our own way. We had a full agenda of girly activities planned: manicures, pedicures, facials, and eyebrow maintenance. We were going the whole hog on our beauty overhaul. And naturally, we had a full DVR of *Sports Wives* to fill the down time.

"Where should we start?" Inga carried a platter of cake pops to the coffee table. I'd given her the cake maker after Emma had accidentally ordered two off the *Late Night Telly Shoppe*. Not my brightest idea, since I was now eating cake pops both at home and at Ull's.

"How about pedicures?" My toes were in no condition to be honeymooning any time soon.

"Excellent." Inga placed her nail caddy on the couch and brought out two bowls filled with warm water. "*Sports Wives* while we soak and pick our colors?"

"You read my mind."

Three episodes later we were putting on our top coats, when there was a pounding at the door. Inga looked up. "Are your flatmates here early?"

"I don't think so. It was so sweet of you to invite them, but they won't be back from Victoria's office party until pretty late." It was more likely they'd stop by for scones in the morning—if they could drag themselves out of bed.

"Well, it's not anybody I know. Gunnar and Ull are fishing, and Olaug always calls before she stops by. And I don't have any other human friends."

The doorbell rang twice in succession. "Impatient, whoever it is," Inga commented. She stood, careful not to disturb the polish on her toes. I giggled as I watched her waddle to the door. "Who is it?" she called through the wood.

"An old friend, come to offer congratulations," a voice barked back.

Inga peered through the peephole and her mouth fell open. "You have to be kidding." She turned to me in shock. "It's Skadi."

"Skadi? My almost-bodyguard? Thor's wanna-be daughter-in-law? That Skadi?"

"That's the one." Inga tapped her foot.

"Inga!"

"What?"

"Don't mess up your toes." Skadi's appearance was alarming, but we'd put a lot of work into our pedicures.

"Oh. Right."

"Open the door, Inga. I know you're standing right there." Skadi's voice was harsh and grating, nothing like Inga's tinkling trill. No wonder Ull didn't want to marry her.

"What do I do?" Inga looked helpless.

"Let her in." I shrugged. "What's she going to do?"

"I can't. Ull was clear—she's top of the no-access list."

"The what?" If Ull had a list of people I wasn't supposed to hang out with, this marked a whole new level of controlling.

"His list. It's for your own good, Kristia. Don't look at me like that."

"There's a list?" I was incredulous.

"Yes, a list." Inga tossed her hair. "Nobody remotely resembling an elf. Nobody I can't identify right away." The knocking on the door interrupted her. "And no Skadi."

"Why no Skadi?"

"Because word around Asgard is she went completely mental when she found out Ull's marrying you. She's all kinds of hung up on him, even after all this time. Her ex-boyfriend, Njord, told Gunnar, who told Ull, who flipped out. With her history of instability—" Inga broke off, clapping her hand to her mouth.

"Let me get this straight. The goddess Thor handpicked for Ull is in love with my fiancé? She's unstable? And Ull knew she was mad at me?" My dream about Skadi had been a vision after all. I sifted through my memory, trying to cherry-pick the most relevant bits from the apparition.

"Well, it hardly matters what Thor wanted, does it? Ull never liked her. Or anyone." That was the mootest of moot points I'd ever heard.

"Inga Andersson, I am here to congratulate the groom and bride-to-be. Now let me in." Skadi's singsong was loud enough for the entire street to hear.

"Oh for goodness sake." I stood and waddled to the door, mindful of my drying polish. "I'll handle this myself."

"Kristia, no." Inga blocked my path. "Ull will kill me."

"I'm strongly considering violence against Ull. Who makes a list of people I'm not allowed to talk to?" *I mean, really?*

"Kristia please," Inga pleaded. "I will get in so much trouble if you open that door."

"Oh Great Odin, this is ridiculous. I just want to wish the happy couple my best." Skadi sounded anything but congratulatory.

"For the thousandth time, Ull is not the boss of me." I gritted my teeth at my friend.

"Inga." The voice coming from outside sounded strained.

I flipped my head over and ran my fingers through the roots to give it volume. Pasting on my finest fake smile, I pushed Inga out of the way and opened the door.

If I'd been expecting the almost-pretty female from my dream, I was about to be disappointed. Skadi was still tall and muscular, and hardly what I would have called feminine, but as I took in the woman who was clearly more goddess than mortal, an unsettling churning formed in the pit of my stomach. The Skadi standing on Inga's porch was much hotter than the one in my mind. Her once-mousy hair was a glossy chestnut that practically bounced across her broad shoulders, and her low-cut top revealed just enough cleavage to make me wonder if Asgardians had access to plastic surgery.

"Skadi?" The woman's appearance was not wasted on Inga. "Is that really you? You're so . . ." For once my verbose friend was at a loss. ". . . so put together."

"Nice of you to notice." Skadi shifted her weight so she was facing me and I could see her muscular quads strain beneath tight jeans. Her movements were strong, powerful, and timed with the precision of a snake poised to strike. She was graceful in the way all Asgardians are, but her mannerisms reminded me more of Gunnar's than Inga's—she lacked the elegance I'd come to expect of a goddess.

And the glint in her eye made it clear she was meaner than a wet mountain lion.

"You were a bigger tomboy than me in school. What happened to you?" Inga's eyes were locked just south of where propriety would have dictated.

"Goddesses change, Inga. I grew up; that's all." And out, by the looks of her chest. I wondered just how familiar Ull was with the improved Skadi. "Besides, I've never been to your adopted realm. I hope I didn't overdo it on the human clothes. I understand these frightfully uncomfortable pants are in style here. I can't imagine why."

"Skinny jeans." Inga nodded in spite of herself. "They're not my favorite either, but they make your legs look amazing when worn with the proper heel." She eyed Skadi's shiny black pumps, which added four inches to her already impressive height. If she towered over me in my dream, she was now positively a giantess. "Those are nice," Inga muttered begrudgingly.

Footwear hardly seemed to matter at the moment. A striking Amazonian immortal was standing in my doorway with a body that could put a supermodel to shame. Every hair was in place, and her face had been made-up with an expert hand. To top it off, the amply-bosomed woman, whose modesty ran on the opposite end of the spectrum from mine, could obviously crush me with her gargantuan lady biceps. The only way to get the better of her would be to out-charm her. It was the one advantage Mormor had given me.

"Hello," I said sweetly, burying my insecurity. "You must be Skadi. Won't you come in?"

Inga seemed to remember her role. She crossed her arms and shook her head at me. "Great, Kristia. Now I have to deal with Ull."

"I'll deal with him, thank you very much," I hissed out of the corner of my mouth. "Have a seat," I gestured toward the couch. "We were just enjoying Inga's treats. Would you care for a cake pop?"

Skadi stared at me. Her eyes moved up and down as she took in every detail of my appearance with latent curiosity. I guess she hadn't had a grandmother who drilled manners into her from the time she could walk. Her loss.

"I have no idea what that is, but sure. I'd love to try a cake pop." Her raspy voice wasn't doing her any favors in the femininity department, but as she crossed the threshold in her four-inch heels, it was clear she was doing her best to work with what she'd been given. She peered at me from under false eyelashes laden with mascara and topped with heavily-glittered lids. I doubted this whole look was for my benefit.

"So." Skadi confirmed my suspicion as she settled herself on the couch. "Is it just the three of us? Or do I get to congratulate the groom-to-be, too?"

"Oh, Gunnar and Ull are out fishing." Inga stayed where she was, arms firmly crossed over her chest. "If you're here to make another pathetic move on Ull, you'll have to wait."

"I'm not here for Ull." Skadi crossed her unnaturally long legs. "I actually wanted to meet you, Kristia."

"How lovely." I sat on the opposite end of the couch and crossed my ankles. "Please help yourself." I gestured to the plate. From the doorway I heard a delicate "harrumph."

"You're here to meet Kristia." Inga stalked over to stand directly behind me. "And why, exactly, are you suddenly interested in her?"

"Oh, Inga." Skadi took a bite of the treat and chewed thoughtfully. "These are good."

"I know," Inga grumbled. "Now why are you here?"

"To welcome Kristia, of course. If the rumors are true, she's going to be one of us."

"Yes. So?"

"So, she'll be the first Asgardian convert . . . ever."

"Not ever." Inga placed her hands on the back of the couch. "Didn't you come from another realm? Come to mention it, you've never told us exactly where you're from."

"Oh, I'm not here to talk about me." Skadi laughed, an awkward chortle that betrayed her discomfort. "I'm here to meet Ull's bride."

"We've established that."

"Well, it's a pleasure to meet you, Skadi," I held my fake smile firmly in place. "Is this really your first time here?"

"It is."

"How are you finding it?"

"Honestly?" Skadi reached for another cake pop. "It's a lot more crowded than I'd thought it would be."

"Well, Cardiff is a pretty big city." I fell into the banter of polite small-talk as calmly as if I were at one of Mormor's bridge parties. "Just an hour's drive from here you'll find the countryside to be much more open—a lot like I imagine Asgard must be."

"That's right, you've never been to Asgard." Skadi brushed an invisible fleck off her flimsy top.

"No. You'll have to tell me about it."

"It's just wonderful. It has much more beauty than anything in this realm."

"Hey." Inga's tone lowered at the thinly-veiled dig.

"Oh, Inga. What I've seen of Midgard is pleasant

enough, but even you can't honestly believe it compares to Asgard. I'm sure you'll agree when you're invited to see it, Kristia."

"I like it here," Inga insisted. "And if you don't, you can just leave."

"Inga," I hissed over my shoulder. "Be nice." If there was one thing I'd learned from watching reality television, it was to never anger a crazy houseguest.

"So is it true, Kristia? Have you really tamed Ull?" Skadi stared at me with doe-eyes, the picture of girlish innocence.

"Well, we're engaged, if that's what you're asking."

"After all these years . . ." Skadi sat back. "I'd never have imagined Ull would fall in love with a human, of all creatures. No offense."

"What's that supposed to mean?" Inga huffed.

"I've got this," I whispered over my shoulder before turning to Skadi. "It's amazing, isn't it? After everything Ull's been through." I kept my tone light. "To think, he's never met anyone who caught his eye."

"That's what they're telling you? Well, he wasn't always a saint." Skadi smirked. "But humans are awfully skittish, as mortal beings go. I can understand why he wouldn't be honest with you. You might run away."

"Oh, you must mean those awful years he spent fighting. He told me all about them. Poor Ull." I forced my face into a sympathetic mask to belie my growing irritation. If Skadi thought she could come in here and undermine our relationship, she didn't have the sense God gave a goose.

"Indeed." Skadi leaned forward. "Aren't you at all nervous to be marrying an assassin? Do you worry that he might hurt you?"

"Ull would never." I shook my head. "He's so sweet with me."

"It doesn't get old? Knowing he can never fully be himself with you?"

"I don't know what you mean, Skadi. Ull's been honest with me since day one. I've never met anyone who's so concerned with making me happy, who wants to take care of me in every possible way." I blushed, thinking of the ways Ull intended to take care of me in the very near future.

Skadi tensed from head to toe, then adjusted her cleavage to its best advantage. "Isn't that nice. Well, I'm so happy for the two of you. You're going to be the first human-born Asgardian. You must be terribly pleased with how things have turned out."

"I am very happy, thank you."

"Anything else?" Inga hadn't moved from her sentinel behind me.

"Why, Inga Andersson, are you kicking me out?" Skadi batted her thick lashes.

"I'm not sure what to make of you today."

"Fair enough." Skadi stood and turned for the door. "Tell Ull I stopped by. You'll have to come over to my place when you're *allowed* in Asgard." She got in her last dig. "If you like these cake pops, you'll love my kransekake."

"You can cook now, too?" Inga's eyes dropped to Skadi's blouse again. "Who are you?"

"I told you, Inga, I've changed. I just want to make Kristia feel welcome, that's all. I remember what it's like to be the new girl."

"Thank you, Skadi. That was very generous of you." I stood and followed her to the porch. "Ull and I will be sure to stop by together when we're in your realm."

"Please do." Skadi was cut off as Inga closed the door.

"Inga! That wasn't nice." But I couldn't help giggling.

"I don't care. That woman is horrible."

"There did seem to be something off about her," I agreed. "But I wouldn't worry too much—the sun doesn't shine on the same dog's tail all the time."

"What does that mean?" Inga asked.

"Just that she'll get what's coming to her."

"I sure as Helheim hope so." Inga grabbed my hand and pulled me toward the couch. "She's usually not that subtle. You should hear the mouth on the *real* Skadi. I couldn't figure out what her game was today. Do you see why she's on the no-access list?"

"Ull was never into her, was he?" I hated to hammer a dead horse, but the image of the busty Amazon woman in body-hugging pants was burning a hole in my brain.

"Oh my goodness, stop asking that. I told you, he's never been into anyone. You're the first girl he's ever loved."

"You realize that's completely unbelievable, right? He's like, a billion years old."

"You greatly underestimate Ull's stubborn streak. He said he wasn't going to fall for anyone, and Odin's ravens, he didn't. Until you." Inga gave me a pointed look.

"Whatever. What was that bit about remembering what it's like to be the new girl? What's her story?" Our visit with Skadi had taken so long our toes were dry. We began applying our first coat to our fingers.

"I wish I knew. We've all wondered how she ended up crazy." Inga carefully painted a deep plum on her little finger. "Her dad died when she was young, and she came to live in Asgard not long after. I'm not all that sure where she came from. It had to be somewhere really awful, the way she acts."

"That's sad." I painted a stripe of white on my thumb. I wanted French tips.

"I think she latched onto the idea of being with Ull, since he'd lost his dad too. And she was always a good fighter. And a good skier. Physically, she is a lot like Ull, but that's where the similarities end. She's a complete basket-case, and Ull does everything he can to live the most structured life possible. He could never have considered her."

"I'm glad." I moved on to my next finger.

"It was kind of fabulous to see you hold your own." Inga giggled. "You didn't let her digs phase you at all."

"Told you I could take care of myself."

"Yes, you can." Inga painted her thumb with a flourish.

"Inga." I appraised my fingers. The French tips were looking pretty good.

"Yes?"

"You know I have to talk to Ull about this no-access thing, right? I can't have him controlling every aspect of my life—especially if he's using you to do it."

"I know." Inga looked up. "But could you maybe wait until I'm out of the house to let him know I told you? I don't want to fight with him this close to the wedding. He might not let me be involved with the planning anymore."

"Organizing it means that much to you?"

"Oh, yes." Inga's smile stretched from ear to ear. "It's not every day you get to see your best friends get married. We've waited for-bloody-ever for Ull to let himself be happy. And getting such a great friend in the process, well, it's just all kinds of fabulous."

When she put it like that, it was hard to be upset at her for following Ull's overbearing orders. But Ull and I definitely needed to have a little chat.

❄ ❄ ❄ ❄

Stewing wasn't an attractive habit, but it was one I'd probably never break. Maybe it was because I had such a long fuse, but once I got angry, irritation crawled into my head and set up a tent. There was no turning it off—even in my sleep. Knowing my penchant for nocturnal imaginings, and knowing how truly frustrated I was with Ull's overprotective behavior, I probably should have just pulled an all-nighter.

But I didn't.

So I shouldn't have been surprised to watch my subconscious-self storm into Ull's bachelor weekend campsite. In the dream it was the middle of the night. I wore cargo pants and combat boots, and I'd smeared black paint beneath my eyes. Apparently I was gearing up for a fight on every possible level.

It should have been funny, but it was downright scary. Everything about my face screamed *fury*, from the deep *V* between my eyes, to the divot beneath my cheekbones, to the harsh set of my jaw. The air was cold thanks to a thick fog resting over the lake, but it crackled with the tension radiating off my skin. As I watched myself march toward Ull's tent, I was surprised by the metallic taste of blood. Only then did I realize I was biting my cheek to keep from shouting.

"Ull Myhr." I stood outside the tent, hands on hips. "Get out here this instant."

There was some shuffling inside the tent. Then Ull poked his head out. His hair was disheveled, his stubble bordering on a full beard. His eyes lit up when he saw me, and he stepped out of the tent, zipping it closed behind him.

"*Hei hei,*" he murmured. He put a hand on the small of my back to draw me in for a kiss.

"Get your hands off me." I shoved him with uncharacteristic strength.

"What did I do?" Ull tilted his head to the side.

"What did you do?" A family of ducks took flight at my tone. Whatever. "You darned well know what you did. What you're doing! You told Inga not to let me around Skadi. You've got a list, *an actual list* of people I can't associate with. You're trying to control my life!"

"Bloody well right I am." Ull spoke so matter-of-factly, I took a step back.

"What?"

"Bloody well right I am." Ull repeated. "You are a mortal, Kristia. You cannot make these kinds of decisions for yourself."

His condescension was grossly out of character, even in a nightmare.

"Who do you think you are? You don't get to decide who I hang out with. If I want to meet Skadi, then I'll meet Skadi. Or whoever else I decide I want to associate with. This is my life, not yours. So back off."

Amusement danced across Ull's perfect face. "Not likely." He pulled a bracelet out of his pocket and attached it to my wrist.

"Jewelry is not going to make this better—ouch! What is this thing? It's pinching me."

"It is a tracker."

"A what?"

"A tracker." Ull patted my head, like I was a confused child. "Tyr—our God of War—uses them to keep tabs on undesirables."

"Did you just call me undesirable?" I tried to rip the bracelet off, but it wouldn't budge. Now my skin burned where it touched me. "What is happening?"

"It is melding to your skin. The pain will wear off in a minute or two."

Tears pricked at my eyes. Ull just tagged me with a skin-melding bracelet? Because I was undesirable? This nightmare stunk worse than the cow patties on the homestead.

"Why would you do this?"

"Because you refuse to understand that when it comes to your safety, I know better than you. The bracelet will track your movements and send them to my phone. If you attempt to go anywhere I have not approved, or fraternize with anyone I do not trust, I will be notified. And I will transport to wherever you are, and stop you."

"You put a GPS on my wrist? Who does that?"

"I do." Ull's eyes darkened. "This is for your own good, Kristia. You just need to trust me."

"You need to trust me!" I cried. "When are you going to start trusting me to handle myself in your world? What do I have to do to prove myself to you?"

The message hit me like a bolt of lightning, and I was sucked out of the field through a vortex in the fog. As the forest whipped past me, I saw Ull frozen by his tent, a shell-shocked expression on his face. That was it, really; that was what all of my frustrations boiled down to.

What did I have to do to prove to Ull that I could handle myself in his world? When would he start believing that I could be everything my prophecy promised I would become?

The vortex changed course so I was flying toward my makeshift bed on Inga's couch. With a jolt I was back to reality, shivering under the thick blankets. My body realized I was awake before my brain did. My hand reached reflexively for my wrist, feeling for the traitorous GPS bracelet. It wasn't there and it never had been. It hadn't been real—it was only a nightmare. Ull would never hurt me. *Ever.*

But it was starting to feel like he might never trust me, either. Forever was an awfully long time to spend with someone if they would never be able to believe in you. It didn't have to happen today, or even next week. Rome wasn't built in a day . . . and I couldn't realistically expect Ull to let go of a lifetime of fears just because we were about to say, "I do."

But I had to know he'd let go eventually. Because whether the GPS bracelet was real or a dream-induced metaphor, I couldn't spend the rest of my existence with someone looking over my shoulder. I had to be free to grow into the goddess everyone expected me to be; the goddess I knew I was meant to become.

I had to be free to be me.

CHAPTER EIGHT

"HELLO DARLING." ULL GREETED me with a warm kiss when he got back the next night. True to form, Inga had dumped Gunnar's luggage in their room and whisked him out of the house to give us some privacy. I hadn't mentioned my dream, but it didn't take a rocket scientist to know I was going to interrogate Ull about his latest overprotective maneuver the minute he walked through the door. Inga was nobody's fool; she wanted to avoid a fight.

"Hi." I kissed Ull back and quickly moved to the couch. "We need to talk."

"Sounds serious." Ull was still in a good mood, obviously relaxed from two days of fishing. "You are not having cold feet?"

"No. But I do have a concern. A big one." *A night-terror level, electroshock-GPS-bracelet-imagining big one.*

"Are you nervous about exams? We have a whole

week left to study, and I am happy to help you prepare. Trust me, Kristia, you will do just fine. You are an exceptional student."

"This isn't about school."

Ull sat next to me on the couch and tucked a strand of hair behind my ear. "Spill."

"Okay. First of all, would you ever put an electroshock bracelet on me to track my moments?"

"What? Why would I do something absurd? Would I happen to be insane in that scenario?"

"I don't know. To protect me?" I bit my bottom lip.

"No. Of course I would never do something that cruel. I would never knowingly hurt you. You know this—or at least, I hope you do. You are my world. Kristia, where is this coming from?"

"Don't ask," I muttered. Then I lifted my chin to stare him down. "Were you going to tell me about your no-access list? Or any other rules you've composed to control my life?"

"Pardon?"

I jumped to my feet and paced in front of the fireplace. "Are you planning to spend the rest of my existence making up arbitrary laws you think will keep me under your thumb, then having our friends enforce them for you? Because that's not the life I want to sign up for."

"Kristia—"

"Why would you think it's okay to control who I spend time with? What I do?" My footsteps fell so hard, the framed photos on the mantel shook.

"You think I want to control you?" Ull furrowed his

brow.

"I know you do!" My frustration piqued—I could feel my eyes burning. "And it's not okay. You set up rules for Inga to enforce, and you didn't even tell me."

"Kristia Tostenson, listen to me right now. I left you in Inga's care. You did not think I would leave your side without making sure you had the best protection possible, did you?"

"Protection?"

"Yes. Protection. You have no idea what will come after you when your identity gets out. So long as you are mortal, there is very little I will not do to keep you safe. Though I would not resort to shock therapy to protect you. Where would you get an idea like that?" Ull shook his head. "I gave Inga a list of people I wanted kept away from you to ensure your safety. What would have happened if Skadi had come around while you were having one of your visions? She is not of sound mind. I do not want her anywhere near you, especially when you are unconscious and unable to defend yourself. I asked Inga to look after you while I was away. And I would do it again."

"Well . . ." I paused. I crossed back to the couch and sat, tucking my knees under my chin. "Fine. I get the list. But I felt really stupid when your crazy ex-lover showed up."

"Skadi was never my lover," Ull corrected fiercely. "And what do you mean she showed up? When was she here?"

"Yesterday. I think she came by to scare me off."

"Did she?"

"Hardly." I rolled my eyes. "It takes a lot more than a manipulative woman to freak me out."

"What did she want?"

"She said she just wanted to congratulate us. But she was wearing an awful lot of makeup for a social call." I waited for Ull to say something, but he'd squeezed his eyes shut.

"Ull? You would never leave me for Skadi, would you? Ull?" I grabbed his face with both hands and stared until he opened his eyes. When he did I could see tears of laughter in their corners.

"I am sorry, my love. I just pictured Skadi in makeup." His shoulders shook with pent-up amusement. "I have changed my mind. I am very glad I was not here to see that. It must have been terrible."

I let out a breath I hadn't realized I was holding. "She is a seriously strange woman."

"I know. And listen to me. I cannot keep saying this. There was never anything between Skadi and me. I want nothing more than for her to stay as far away from you and me as possible. Do you understand?" I sat back against the cushions, relieved I didn't have any real competition from the goddess in the skimpy top.

"What concerns me is why she was here. I do not believe for one minute she wanted to offer congratulations. Skadi is not stable, Kristia. Who knows what she could have done if something had set her off? You should have listened to Inga and left her outside," Ull growled, his irritation renewed. "How am I supposed to keep you out of harm's way if you defy every safeguard I have set in place for you?"

I shoved my hand through my hair with annoyance. It always came back to this. "That's what I keep telling you. I don't need to be constantly looked after. I took care of her myself."

"This time. But what if she'd been in a darker place? You do not understand what Skadi is capable of." Ull stared out the window.

"That's on you—you never told me about her. I can't protect myself from dangers I don't know are out there." Or from an irate deity with a personality that could tick off the Pope.

"I do not want you to protect yourself. Inga, Gunnar and I are much stronger than you, at least for now. We can take far better care of you."

"I get that. But at some point in this relationship you are going to have to start trusting me." We stared at each other for a long time. I was seriously frustrated.

Ull reached for my hand. "I know you are upset. I am sorry I was not upfront with you."

"You have to start trusting me," I pleaded for what felt like the hundredth time.

"I know," Ull whispered. "But it scares me. If anything ever were to happen to you . . ."

"I get it. I do," I conceded. "But this marriage is never going to work if you don't let me share all of your world—the good *and* the bad."

"All right. I will." Ull drew a breath. "Please know that I have every confidence in you. At the same time, I have no confidence in the worlds around you. There is nothing you cannot accomplish once you set your stubborn little mind to it, and nobody knows that better than me. But you have to understand that what you see as overbearing, I see as protecting you. I will do whatever it takes to keep you safe. You are my reason for living."

"I know. And you're mine." I cupped his cheek in my hand. "And so long as you start being *honest with me*," I stressed the last words, "we are going to be just fine."

"I know we are." Ull leaned in and planted a gentle kiss on my neck. I nestled my head on his shoulder and closed my eyes. It had been a long week.

❄ ❄ ❄ ❄

"You have enough pens?" Ull stared at my desk. It was the day of our Mythology final, and we were waiting on Professor Carnicke's word to begin.

"You can never be too prepared." I snuck a glance at Ull's desk. It was empty, except for his exam notebook and a single writing instrument.

"But seven pens? Seriously, Kristia. Five pens might give out on you, but surely not six."

There was barely time to give Ull my most irritated glare before Professor Carnicke stepped up to the podium. "And, begin," she announced. She clicked the overhead projector to *on*, bringing our final exam topic to the white screen.

Citing references from myths of each culture we studied this year, what themes most resonate with today's society? Which, if any, are obsolete?

I whipped the notebook open and clicked pen

number one.

Themes. Common themes. Creation, naturally, played a part in each culture's mythology. Who we were and where we'd come from was a red-letter question even thousands of years ago.

The afterlife was big too. Every society had wanted reassurance that there was more to our existence than the mortal realm. My teeth grazed the tip of my pen. Those were too obvious. At least half my classmates would hit on those themes, and even if I dropped bits from the Greek, Indian, Egyptian, Celtic and Norse lessons we'd had, my essay would still get lost in the crowd. I needed something original—something that would make me stand out from the hundred other students. Something Professor Carnicke had never seen before . . .

The seat next to me squeaked as Ull shifted his considerable form. He wrote lazily in his booklet, seemingly unconcerned with crafting an earth-shattering, original essay. Meanwhile, I was so obsessed with making top marks in my classes that I was a knotted mess of barely-brushed hair and yesterday's sweatpants. My fingers were cramped so tightly around pen number one that my knuckles locked up. Shifting the pen to my mouth, I realized my lower lip was practically raw from my worrying it. I also realized the pen was clicking against my teeth. Apparently the three energy drinks I'd downed after my all-nighter had made me jittery. Next to me, Ull drew a calm breath and continued writing. Of course he could be relaxed—thanks to his blind faith in those ridiculous prophecies, he knew exactly how the rest of his existence was going to unfold. He didn't have to worry about impressing professors or acing exams, or what he was going to do when he graduated. Besides worrying about Ragnarok, he never questioned where his life was going or what was coming next. He didn't have to—he had Norns to do that for him.

Without warning, the exam room disappeared. Now, I was in a small wooded grove. Ferns and ivy laced the ground surrounding a small pond, with a positively massive tree rising from the other side of the water. Three tiny women moved toward the tree, each clad in a filmy ivory gown. On closer inspection, I could see they were pouring water on the tree's roots.

Yggdrasil. The world tree. This must be the home of The Three Sisters. Which made those three women . . . The Fates.

One of the women reached into the air. Sunlight danced off her deep burgundy hair as she moved, flecks of crimson reflecting in the pond's still surface. A piece of parchment appeared in her fingers, and she pulled it to her. She unrolled the scroll, and stared at the page. Her sisters continued to bring water to the tree, one bucket at a time.

The woman holding the pail lifted her eyes. "What does it say, Skuld?"

"I . . . I don't know." Skuld shook her head. "The page is turning blank."

"Blank?" Her sisters ran to her side. They stared at the parchment as if it were infected. "What's wrong with it?"

"Something is erasing the prophecy." Skuld held the paper to the sky. Sunlight filtered down through Yggdrasil's leaves, bathing the sisters in a mottled glow.

"This has never happened before," one of the women whispered. Her strawberry hair tumbled at her shoulders.

The third sister wrung her hands together. "What does it mean?"

"I don't know." Skuld twirled the parchment between her fingertips. "But what if it's not just this prophecy? What if they all disappear?" She clutched her throat. "What are we going to do if we can no longer see what is coming?"

The women stared at each other in horror as I was sucked out of the vision, through the forest, and back to the brightly-lit examination room.

The beauty of the vision hit me like a runaway freighter with busted breaks, and my fingers relaxed their death-grip on the pen. The prophecies were changing. *I* was changing. The dark end the Sisters had predicted for Asgard wasn't set in stone anymore. Despite their all-knowing powers, they hadn't seen me coming years ago, and they couldn't see what I was going to do now. The truth was, nobody could ever really know exactly how the future would unfold. And more importantly, there was no *reason* to know. Ull had shut himself off for who-knows how many years because some stupid prophecy told him he was fated to die at Ragnarok. But I was proof that everything could change. Here I was, normal old Kristia Tostenson from Nehalem, and out of nowhere it became my job to save the realms from imminent destruction. That hadn't been The Fates' plan for me, and yet here I was. My long ago words came flying back at me.

Sometimes finding your destiny means doing the opposite of what The Fates have in store.

Without another glance at the magnificent deity coolly scribbling beside me, and without so much as a roman numeral in an outline, I started to write. Words flowed to paper in an unbroken stream, my subconscious purging months of frustration. In a lot of ways, it was nice to know what was coming. At least in Asgard it created order, and allowed their society to function with minimal internal disturbance. But it came with a cost—look at the agony knowing his future had caused Ull. And what good was knowledge if it stopped you from living?

My pen pressed across the notebook so hard I was afraid it might tear the paper. Easing my grip, I continued to write, fleshing out my argument with references from the Celtic and Egyptian myths, and touching on the significance of the Oracle at Delphi. When I circled back to the Norse Norns, I gripped my pen so tightly it snapped in two. The top half landed on Ull's notebook. He picked it up with a surprised smirk, and set it gently to the side.

"Superhuman strength kicked in a little early, *ja*? Guess you did need all those extras."

"Shh." I picked up pen number two. It got me through the rest of the hour, and when Professor Carnicke called time I set it down with a flourish. It might not have been the most eloquent exam submitted that day, but it was sure to be the most passionate . . . and the most personal.

"Well, that was fun." Ull clasped his hands together, raising his arms high above his head. The thin fabric of his cashmere sweater strained against his biceps, earning more than one appreciative stare from the sea of girls seated around him.

They could stare all they wanted. Next week he'd be all mine.

The thought left a warm buzz in the pit of my belly. The three energy drinks zeroed in on the spot, sending a chorus of tap dancing crickets across my lower abdomen. They hoofed out a rhythm to the delicious thought. *All mine, all mine, all mine.*

"And now we can celebrate." Ull followed me out of the row, placing his hand on the small of my back as he guided me out of the classroom. "Happy birthday, sweetheart."

"Thanks." I grinned. "Finishing the last exam of my sophomore year—not a bad way to celebrate."

"I have a better one. Though you probably need to crash after your all-nighter."

"That obvious, huh?" I smoothed my messy ponytail.

"Not at all." Ull squeezed the side of my hip as we walked. The familiar gesture redirected what little blood was left in my head to somewhere considerably more agitating. "It is two o'clock now. Let me walk you home. You can rest for a few hours while I tend to some arrangements, then I will send Gunnar to pick you up at six. We can have a proper celebration then."

"Send Gunnar? Why don't I just meet you at your place? What's going on?"

"That, my darling, is highly-classified intel. You would not want to ruin your birthday surprise."

I would, actually. Surprises tended to freak me out. "Will you at least tell me what to wear?"

"Victoria knows. Do as she tells you." Ull steered me in the direction of my flat as I chewed on this nugget.

"So I can just drag it out of Victoria then?"

"Mortals . . ." Ull chuckled. "Always have been the most impatient creatures. Just do what Victoria says and get ready for the birthday night of your life."

The crickets took a bow and began a frenzied encore to their new theme song. *Night of your life, night of your life.*

"You know there's no way I'm going to be able to sleep after that comment," I complained.

"You will sleep. There is an all-nighter and an energy-drink crash on sleep's side." Ull leaned down to whisper in my ear. "Besides, you want to be well rested for what I have planned."

Thousands of nerve endings snapped to military attention. My head swam with visions of what Ull might *have planned.* By the time we entered the courtyard of the student houses, I was an even bigger bundle of nerves than I'd been before our Mythology exam. Hot bejeebus, that god could push my buttons.

"Get some sleep, Kristia." Ull kissed me softly. He stroked my cheek with the back of one finger, then backed slowly toward the fountain. "Gunnar will be here in four hours."

"'Kay," I called feebly after him. When he rounded the corner, I shoved my key in the lock and stumbled into the flat. Suddenly, four hours seemed like forever.

CHAPTER NINE

"HOLY MOTHER, KRISTIA. YOU look hot."

"You don't have to sound so surprised." I elbowed Gunnar in the ribs as I closed my front door. My four-inch heels wobbled precariously on the cobblestone path, hindered, no doubt, by the absolutely enormous gown Victoria had put me in. It was spectacular—pale pink lace, layers of crinoline supporting the full skirt, and a strapless neckline that more than showed off some artfully enhanced . . . assets. I wasn't sure what boggled me more—that Victoria had whipped up an Oscar-worthy gown on two weeks' notice, or that she expected me to be able to walk in the sky high heels she'd paired it with.

"Hold my arm." Gunnar watched me stumble across the stones with barely contained glee. "He'll kill me if I have to take you to the emergency room instead of the castle."

'The castle? We're going to a castle?" My face lit up. What a great birthday. A date at a castle!

"*Dritt.* That was supposed to be a secret. Well,

whatever. I can still make this night a surprise." Gunnar helped me into his Jeep. He had to—it was one of those ten feet tall things, with headlights on top. Where he went off-roading in urban Wales was beyond me, but this was clearly not a vehicle meant for surface streets.

Or for ball gowns.

After a fairly awkward struggle, I was situated in the truck. Gunnar closed the door behind me and climbed into the driver's side. Turning, he rooted through the messy backseat. "Gym shoes. Jump-rope. Textbook—don't need that anymore. Ah, there it is."

"A tie? That's going to look a little weird with your hoodie, don't you think?"

"Have a little faith, Kristia. Close your eyes."

I did as instructed, and I felt the silky fabric cover my brow. "What are you doing?"

"Hold still." Gunnar pushed the tie over my eyes and tugged, binding it tightly in place. "Perfect. Now you won't know *which* castle we're going to."

"You could have just told me not to tell Ull you squealed." I pointed out.

"Yeah. But this is more fun." Gunnar laughed as he threw the Jeep into gear. I felt the hum of the engine as we drove down the street.

"What are you and Inga doing this summer?" I asked. It felt rude to talk without looking at him, but Gunnar's tie made that kind of difficult.

"Besides attending the wedding of the millennium?" From under my blindfold, I imagined him shooting me that enormous smile, the one that made his dimple pop out. "We're going to do some scuba diving off the Maldives. There's some kind of migration going on right now that's supposed to be out of this world."

"You guys are so brave. I could never go scuba diving."

"Why not? It rocks."

"I don't believe in stepping down a rung on the food chain."

"Meaning?" Gunnar braked so hard my head nearly hit the window. "Sorry. Rogue cat."

"Meaning I'm pathologically afraid of sharks. Also sting rays. And sunfish."

Gunnar's laugh filled the car. "You're willing to go through whatever they're going to do to you to turn you immortal, but you're afraid of a couple of fish?"

"Sharks. And sting rays. And maybe also fish."

"You are something else." The laughter ebbed. "Ull's gonna have his hands full with you."

"Says the guy who wants to go diving with sharks."

"You'll come around." Gunnar spoke confidently. "Once you realize sharks can't hurt you, you'll be begging us to go on holiday. Just wait."

"You're an adrenaline addict." It wasn't a question. If there was one thing I'd learned during the past nine months, it was that Gunnar felt most alive when he was hurtling toward what the rest of us would see as certain death. He and Inga were perfect for each other.

"Y.O.L.O., you know?"

"Yeah, but the 'once' *you* only live is forever."

"Po-tay-toe, po-tah-toe." Gunnar seemed to steer

to the side as the sound of a siren neared. "Uh-oh, must be an accident. I'll pull over."

The siren got louder, and by the time Gunnar stopped the car it was blaring so intently I figured it must have been directly behind us.

"What's going on?" I craned my neck, even though the tie blocked my vision. "Is there an accident?"

"Get out of the car and keep your hands where I can see them!" The angry voice was undermined by the perpetually polite Welsh accent. It came from just outside the Jeep—whatever was happening, it was close.

"Aw, *dritt,*" Gunnar muttered.

"Ooh, who's in trouble?" I strained against the blindfold. "Can I take this thing off? I can't see."

"Out of the car, now!"

I heard the car door open and I wondered if Gunnar was getting out of the car to help the officers. Horns honked around us, heightening the air of confusion. "Gunnar?"

"Sorry, Kristia. This will only take a minute." Gunnar sounded further away, now he was outside of the Jeep. Something smacked against the hood and I felt the car shake.

Enough with Ull's surprise. The blindfold was coming off.

Before I could tear the tie from my eyes, someone opened my door. Thick arms reached across to unbuckle my seatbelt, and I was physically removed from the truck. My feet kicked against my captor's hold, but he cradled me tightly against his chest. "It's all right, miss. You're safe now."

Safe from what?

"Let go of me!" My voice sounded shrill. I pounded against a chest that felt like it was made of lead until my feet touched the pavement. Immediately I ripped the blindfold from my eyes and glared. A uniformed man with a chest like a boulder stared back at me. "What do you think you're doing?"

"Saving your life, miss. Did he hurt you?"

"Did who hurt me?" I stared at my misguided savior, perplexed. He was a clean-cut man in his late twenties with dark hair and grey eyes. His police uniform looked freshly pressed, and he carried a baton tucked into his waistband.

"The perp, miss. Did he hurt you before he abducted you?"

"Abducted me? What are you talking about?" I followed the officer's stare to the front of the Jeep, where an officer had Gunnar's face pressed against the hood. His hands were behind his back in handcuffs, and he was looking at me with barely contained amusement. My fingers stroked the silk tie lying against the bodice of my gown.

Everything came together. "You think he abducted me?" The laugh escaped without warning, tiny bubbles dancing through the air as I processed the absurdity of the situation. Me in a ball gown, blindfolded by a silk tie. And Gunnar in his hoodie and jeans, driving his off-roading vehicle well beyond the speed limit through the streets of Cardiff. "You think *he* abducted *me*!" The laugh built, until I was bent over, my arms clutching my ribs. "This. Is. Fabulous."

"Kristia? You want to help me out here?" My assassin friend's face was still pushed up against the Jeep's hood. Another guffaw escaped my lips.

"Do you know this man?" Officer Grey Eyes stared at me in confusion.

"Yes." I choked back my laughter. "He's my friend. He's taking me to meet my fiancé, who wants to surprise me because it's my birthday."

"So the blindfold . . ." Grey Eyes' pale face turned pink.

"It's so I don't see where we're going. He's not kidnapping me. Honest."

"Let him go," Grey Eyes called to his partner. "It's not what we thought."

"You sure?" The officer smashing Gunnar's face seemed reluctant to release his hold. Judging by his sizeable midsection and undesirable hairline, I surmised he enjoyed having someone like Gunnar under his thumb.

"You are telling the truth, right, miss? Because if you're in any kind of trouble now is the time to speak up. We can help." Grey Eyes watched carefully for my reaction.

"I swear it's fine. I'm marrying his best friend. He's practically family." I held up my fingers in the scout's salute.

"All right." Grey eyes pressed a card into my hand. "We'll just need you to sign something. And if you have any trouble, call me. My badge number is on the card."

"Thanks." I fought against the laughter rising in my

throat. It would have to wait until we were on the road again. Grey Eyes already looked embarrassed enough.

"Let us know if you need any further assistance, miss." Grey Eyes held out a yellow form. I scribbled my signature and he backed away, but not before I caught him staring at my cleavage.

"Thank you," I called, pointedly. When he realized he'd been caught staring, he hurried toward his squad car. His partner released Gunnar with a clipped apology, and in seconds the officers were speeding away.

This was going to make one heck of a story.

"Now that that's out of the way," Gunnar muttered. He rubbed at his wrists, sending me into a fresh wave of hilarity. My amusement came in undignified guffaws now. I might have even snorted. "What a night."

"Hey, Gunnar. Remember that time Ull asked you to look out for me and you *got yourself arrested?"* I hooted.

"Shut up, Kristia." But the dimple was out.

"Wait until Inga hears this!"

Gunnar rested his head against the steering wheel. "Is there any chance we can keep this little episode between us?"

"Nope."

"Yeah, I figured." Gunnar raked his fingers through his unkempt hair. "Well, don't say I never showed you a good time."

"Oh, if there's one thing I'm sure of it's that Gunnar Andersson knows how to show a girl a good time. So good it should be illegal!" My sides ached from laughter, but I couldn't stop myself.

"You know it." Gunnar grinned. "Now are you going to laugh at me all night, or do you want to see your fiancé? He'll be pretty irked if I don't get you there in the next ten minutes."

"Can you do that? How much further is it?" I dabbed at the corners of my eyes.

"Doesn't matter." Gunnar's dimple deepened. "Hold on, girl. I'm gonna take you for a *ride*."

❄❄❄❄

Eight minutes and one terrifying car ride later, we pulled up to Castell Coch. The stone structure rose from a sea of trees, protected on all sides by oaks and willows and ferns in every imaginable shade of green. Its grey turrets rose from the foliage, topped with flags that shifted gently in the evening breeze.

"I know this place." I smiled slowly. "Ull took me here when we first started dating. Before . . ." *Before I knew he was a god.*

"Yep. Wanted to celebrate your birthday with a trip down memory lane. Sort of." Gunnar stepped out of the Jeep and crossed to my side. He opened my door and leaned down. "Hey, if you could forget to mention what happened tonight to Ull . . ."

"Not a chance." I giggled. The story of Gunnar in handcuffs was way too good to keep to myself. "It was the high point of my week."

"Evading arrest was the high point of your week? You have some seriously messed up ideas of fun."

"I didn't nearly get arrested. You did," I pointed

out. "And yes. Watching you talk your way out of jail time was all kinds of fun."

"You're a lot meaner than you look." Gunnar appraised me from an angle. "I like this side of you."

"Thanks."

Gunnar's green eyes sparkled, our faces mirroring our amusement. So far, my nineteenth birthday was turning out to be nothing like I'd expected.

"Well unless you wanna give the law another run for their money, I believe someone's waiting for you." Gunnar jutted his chin toward the steps. My eyes moved up the stone path. Every third stair was bookended with iron lanterns, each holding a blazing pillar candle. A light dusting of white petals marked the center of the path, and at the top was a vision the likes of which I'd never forget. Ull stood calmly, his hands folded behind his back and his feet shoulder width apart. He wore a jet-black tuxedo that made the silvery-blue of his eyes pop even more than usual. His normally disheveled hair was slicked back so it looked almost wet, and he was staring at me with a look that made everything around me slow to a standstill.

Good night nurse, that god was beautiful. And by some inexplicable twist of fate, he was mine. *Thank you, fate.*

"See you later, Kristia. Don't do anything I wouldn't do. Or better yet, do. Odin knows Ull needs it." Gunnar's words registered somewhere in the lump of Jell-O that had become my brain.

"See you." I might have spoken out loud; I wasn't sure. Because at that moment, my living, breathing, testosterone-oozing Norse god was descending the staircase. When he reached my side he held out an arm. My fingers wrapped around the soft fabric of his jacket, a finely-threaded wool that was smooth under my hand. Without a word, Ull raked his eyes up my body. They grazed the line of the full, flowing skirt; they admired the way the dress nipped just below my hips and clung to my bottom, maintaining its fit through the bust. They lingered at the sweetheart neck of the strapless gown with the appropriate amount of appreciation. Victoria had used a clever combination of built-in pads and tape—*tape!* —to ensure my assets would have their moment in the sun.

They did. Several moments, to be precise.

"Kristia." Ull let out a throaty groan. "When I asked Victoria to make you a dress I had no idea she would try to kill me with it."

"You like it?" I moved my hips so the skirt swished around my feet.

"Like is not the word for what I feel about that dress. Or rather, you in that dress. Any possibility you want to cut this evening short?"

"Not a chance." I squeezed his arm. "I've never worn anything like this before. I might never take it off."

"Never? Well that's just no fun." Gunnar chuckled from behind me. I'd totally forgotten he was still here, but there he was, leaning casually against the car. Smirking.

"That will do." Ull dismissed his friend with a wave of his hand. His eyes never left my chest.

"No gratitude, mate. I swear, the things I put up with for you . . ."

"Goodnight Gunnar," I called sweetly. "Thanks for the ride."

"Whatever." Gunnar's cheeky tone carried through the air. "See you back at home, Ull. Or not."

The hum of the engine grew quieter as Gunnar pulled down the drive. When the only sounds were the thrum of the crickets and the light rustle of leaves in the warm breeze, Ull tore his gaze away from Victoria's pièce de résistance. "Shall we?"

"We shall."

With careful steps, Ull led me up the staircase. The hem of my dress brushed the stones, and I was terrified I'd catch a toe and take an Olympic-level tumble. But by some miracle, I reached the top unscathed.

My fingers gripped Ull's forearm as we made our way up the cobblestone path to the heavy wooden doors. They were open, light blazing from inside like a welcoming beacon.

"After you." Ull gestured for me to go ahead of him, and I entered the foyer, my curiosity piqued. The last time we'd been here this late he'd had to sweet-talk a guard to get us on the property. What had he had to do to get the castle to open on a Tuesday night?

Ull placed a hand on the small of my back and gently guided me to the second story. We stepped into a small room, and recognition dawned. It was so romantic. So over-the-top. So generous.

It was so typically Ull.

"You rented out Castell Coch for my birthday." My lips curved up as I dipped my head. Blonde curls tumbled across my face, providing a welcome shield. Without needing to see my cheeks I knew I was one hundred shades of red.

Ull stepped in front of me. He gathered my hair in one hand and gripped it behind my neck. He rested his forehead against mine, pressing lightly so I was forced to lift my head. Our eyes locked, and the heat pouring out of his gaze sent a stream of warmth straight through me. Blood seeped from my cheeks and traveled down, gathering somewhere else entirely. It wasn't an altogether unpleasant feeling. Nothing with Ull ever was.

"You only turn nineteen once." Ull brushed his thumb against my bottom lip. I felt the touch in more than one place. My hand moved to his chest, a collection of muscles concealed beneath his pocket square. He tensed against my hand before stepping closer. His thigh pressed against mine in a way that made cohesive speech impossible, and the hand not holding my hair made its way down my back. It brushed the bare skin at my shoulder blades, fiery shivers radiating from the contact down the backs of my arms. He moved his hand lower, caressing the curve of my spine with unbearable slowness. When his lips finally met mine, I moved against him, desperate to erase even the half-inch between us. Every touch sent sparks of heat flying across my oversensitive skin. If this went on much longer, I could actually burst into flames.

Ull's hand continued its slow trajectory, pausing where he usually stopped at my hip. I stepped closer, so only a few layers of fabric separated us. *Don't stop. Please.*

Ull let out a groan. "*Faen*." The word sent a fresh wave of blood somewhere not far from where his hand was resting. Without warning Ull released his hold. Disappointment coursed through me as I realized I'd pushed him too far. But before I could break our kiss, his hands were back, cupping my backside through the lacy fabric of my gown. He caressed the muscles with his palms, all the while plunging his tongue deep into my mouth. I was overwhelmed by the assault on my senses, and I gave myself over to the feelings awakening in my body. Ull had kissed me before, but never like this. Desire flooded my belly, and I dug my nails into his back. I clawed at his jacket, at the felonious fabric separating us, all the while drinking in the intoxicating taste of his tongue against mine. Ull's hands moved faster, his kisses grew more intense, until he wrapped his fingers around my biceps. He lifted me in one determined move, separating our bodies so quickly my head fell forward.

Dang it.

"Too much?" I panted, avoiding his gaze. If I caught him giving me that *get over here* look again, I'd be a goner.

"We have company."

My head snapped to attention and for the first time I noticed a vested waiter standing by the door.

"My apologies." He cleared his throat nervously. "But dinner is ready on the balcony."

"The balcony?" I smoothed the front of my dress as Ull straightened his jacket.

"Right this way." The waiter shuffled across the room, his face crimson. Ull laced his fingers through mine and we followed him through the open door. Outside, a table set with white linen and china was flanked by two blazing heat lamps. Candles lined the wall, casting shadows over the brown stones of the façade. A low arrangement of white roses sat in the center of the table.

"Birthday girl." Ull held out a chair with a smile.

"Thank you." I flushed. When he had adjusted my chair, Ull took the seat across from me. Our still-blushing waiter lifted the silver domes from our plates, and disappeared with barely a "*bon appetit*."

"I think we embarrassed him." Ull smiled.

"You think?" I ran my fingers through my hair, hoping I didn't look as fired up as I felt.

"Happy birthday, darling." Ull raised his glass. Pink liquid bubbled in the flute. It still caught me off guard that the drinking age in Wales was eighteen.

"Happy graduation. Again." I raised my own glass and we toasted. The champagne tickled my throat. "Is this the one we drank the night you proposed?"

"One and the same. Someday I'll take you to the winery. It is in Napa, a little chateau up on a hillside. Just gorgeous."

"I can't wait."

We tucked into our plates, spending a good few

minutes savoring our food. Our table was small so that Ull's knees rested against mine, and the tension between us made it impossible to actually taste anything.

I was pretty sure Ull had chosen filet mignon for my birthday meal, though it was entirely possible I was eating chicken nuggets. My brain was singularly focused on Ull's leg brushing mine, his fingers tapping the tablecloth, and his eyes searing straight into my soul. If I read his expression correctly, eating was the last thing he wanted to be doing too.

Jeez, this gown felt tight.

"Have you given any thought to what you want to do next term?" Ull filled my champagne glass. Long fingers brushed against mine as he returned the bottle to the ice bucket, sending hot shivers racing up my arm.

And warm. The gown was starting to feel a little warm.

"Be . . . married?"

"Well of course, that." Ull laughed quietly. "I mean with school. I kind of assume you want to stay on in Wales, though if you were thinking about returning to your college in Oregon I could talk to Olaug about procuring a property there. Or you could take an indefinite leave of absence and just let me spoil you."

My cheeks flamed. "Umm . . . I know don't want to go back to Oregon."

"Fair enough. Do you want to re-enroll at Cardiff? Or are you thinking of taking some time off?"

Truth be told, I hadn't given a lick of thought to my

junior year. I'd been too preoccupied with getting married and getting my admission ticket to Asgard to think beyond May. But registration would be closing soon. If I wanted to finish my degree, I needed to sign up for some units. And I did want to finish my degree . . . didn't I? It was part of my five-year plan—graduate, get a job as junior curator, maybe find a boyfriend who didn't think I was loonier than a two-headed bat . . . Lord, my five-year plan was outdated.

"Kristia? Are you okay?" Ull stared at me from across the table.

"Uh-huh." Five-year plan my foot, *none* of the things on last year's to-do list were even relevant anymore. I was marrying a Norse deity, ending my human life, becoming an honest-to-goodness goddess, and, if everything went according to plan, saving the worlds from imminent destruction. How exactly *did* junior year factor into all of that?

"You have your thinking face on." Ull furrowed his brow. "It is cute. And often leads to trouble."

"Sorry." I rubbed my lips together and forced my brows to a neutral position. "I just kind of forgot about registering. I think I want to finish school—I've never not finished anything, so it would feel wrong to drop out. But I'm also not sure what our life is going to look like three months from now. You know?"

"The blessing and the curse of being of Asgard. You never know what tomorrow is going to look like." Ull reached across the table to touch my cheek. "How about this. We can get you registered, and see how you feel in the fall."

"Buy some more time, huh?" My hand covered his, the touch sweltering against my face.

"You will find we tend to establish a multitude of contingencies. For instance, Gunnar and Inga have enrolled at your former college *and* the University of Wales. We did not know where you would feel most comfortable transitioning to our life, and we wanted to make sure you had options."

"Really?" My eyes pricked. "They'd uproot their lives for me?"

"It is what we do for each other. We are a family." Ull's words pushed the tears over the edge. "This makes you cry?"

"It's just so different from what I'm used to." I pressed my fingers to the corners of my eyes to stop the moisture. "Mormor would have done anything for me, and I felt the same about her. But my parents . . ."

"I am sorry they are not coming to our wedding. It truly is their loss. If it is any consolation, the Myhrs are thrilled you are becoming one of us. My mother cannot wait to gain a daughter."

"And I can't wait to meet Sif. I'll bet she's amazing."

Ull placed his napkin on the table and stood up. He removed his jacket, then crossed to stand beside me. "Shall we take a walk, Miss Tostenson?"

"Absolutely."

"Put this on. There are no heat lamps on the grounds." He helped me into his tuxedo coat before guiding me down the stone steps. When we reached the grass, he laced his fingers through mine. We walked in silence; only the sounds of nighttime birds, stirring crickets, and our gentle footsteps broke the calm. Ull tightened his grip when I stumbled. "Are you all right?"

"Hold on." I bent to remove my shoes. My toes might freeze, but the death traps had to go. "Even if they weren't a trip hazard, I doubt the groundskeeper wants me aerating his lawn."

"Always thinking of others." Ull kissed the top of my head while I gathered my shoes and my skirt in the hand that wasn't holding his. "I love that about you."

"I love a lot of things about you." I tilted my head to gaze at him. He was magnificent in the moonlight. The sharp line of his jaw was peppered with his signature stubble, and his normally pale eyes were almost an inky blue in the darkness. They did that sometimes—shifted with his mood. They'd been this color once at Ýdalir. And again tonight . . .

"Do you remember the first time I brought you here?" The inky-blue eyes zeroed in on mine.

"I do," I whispered. That kiss in the woods was something I would *never* forget.

"Me too." One corner of Ull's mouth turned up. "Why do you think we are here?" Without another word he scooped me in his arms and carried me into the forest. My hands clasped around his neck—his arms were thick as two wooden planks, but the speed with which he ran still made me nervous. I shouldn't have worried. In ten seconds flat he had me backed against the tree where he'd first administered his earth-shattering kiss. At least, I think it was the same tree. My brain wasn't exactly operating on all cylinders.

His lips moved against mine with delicious slowness at the same time as he held my wrists over my head. The bark felt rough against the back of my head but I didn't care. Being sandwiched between a tree and a Norse god was more than worth it. His tongue tasted minty as it danced against mine. And his hips . . . *sweet mother of pearl* . . .

"Oh!" I let out a surprised gasp as Ull's mouth moved to my neck. His tongue massaged my skin and his teeth took small bites. The hand not holding my wrists trailed a line down the arm of the too-big jacket I wore. Ull's fingers pushed the lapel aside and brushed the upper seam of my dress. My skin tingled, a thousand tiny shockwaves bouncing across my torso as I waited to see what he'd do next.

I leaned into him, desperate to prolong the touch. As I did, Ull moved against me in a way that made me forget all sense.

Please. Don't. Stop.

Ull raised his head at the sound of my whimper. He squeezed his eyes shut, and took a step back. He eased his finger away, placing his hand firmly around my waist. I whimpered again, but this time for a different reason. Ull stared at me with eyes that were still that inky blue. His face mirrored my frustration, even as he pressed his forehead to mine and murmured, "Dessert is ready."

"Dessert?"

Ull tilted his head to the ground. For the first time I noticed a picnic blanket flanked by votive candles. A chocolate cake, silver ice bucket, and a bottle of *Brut Rosé* sat on the edge of the blanket. It was a perfectly thoughtful birthday dessert.

Only it wasn't the dessert I wanted.

It took everything I had not to let out a petulant cry. *But it's my birthday* would have made me sound like a five year old.

Still . . . as Ull helped me onto the ivory blanket, I wasn't thinking about cake or champagne. There was only one thought making its way across my hormone-addled brain.

I hoped the inky-blue eyes were here to stay.

CHAPTER TEN

"WE MADE IT." ULL squeezed my shoulders gently.

"This year went by so fast." It was graduation day, and I was standing on Ull's porch, trying not to freak out about meeting his mom.

"They adore you." Ull stroked the knot in my neck and I melted into him.

"Right."

"They do. Thor thinks you are already a part of the family, and my mother is convinced you must walk on water. I am inclined to agree."

"Stop it." I blushed.

"Come." He lifted a strand of my hair and leaned down to kiss the side of my neck. "They are waiting."

When he opened the door, I discovered my legs wouldn't move. The Goddess of Beauty stood beaming on the other side. She was the picture of physical perfection.

"*Hei hei,* Kristia. So lovely to meet you. We have been waiting a long time for you to come along." She held out her hand, but I was too nervous to move.

Mormor would never have tolerated such rudeness.

"Oh, you poor thing." Sif swept in with a soft hug. She tossed her long gold hair as she pulled back, and the air suddenly smelled like heather. "We must be a lot to take in. Come, sit."

Sif wrapped an arm around my waist and walked me to the couch. She moved so gracefully she could have made Inga look clumsy. "Tell me, sweetie, are you ready to be done with school? It must be a relief to be finished with your exams."

"Yes Mrs. Myhr. It's nice to be done studying." I crossed my ankles as I sat.

"Oh please, call me Sif." She patted my hand affectionately. "No point in being formal. You are family now."

The warmth in her voice was soothing.

"And you, son? Are you finally done studying, or will you be starting on your twenty-first Master's soon?"

Ull took the spot next to me on the couch. My mouth opened just a little. He had twenty degrees?

"Mother," he admonished.

"Well?" Sif lifted her chin. "I am proud of my boy." Turning to me she stage-whispered, "He also has doctorates in law, medicine, biology, and a post-doctorate in environmental sciences."

"Really?" I gaped at him. "*Dr.* Myhr? Why didn't you tell me?"

"I do not want you to think of me as an old man."

"Oh yeah, because I was pretty sure you were only

twenty-one in human years." Ull laughed with me. Just then Thor walked through the front door, holding a bag from one of Ull's favorite takeout restaurants. His fiery-red hair, battle-worn skin, and intimidating frame still gave me butterflies. It was just unreal to be in the same room as the actual God of Thunder. Thor returned my shy smile with a dignified wave.

"Oh, Kristia," Sif's lilting voice trilled with happiness as she looked at her husband. "Thor and I are so pleased that Ull has chosen you. It was hard for us to watch his heart close and know there was nothing we could do to stop it."

I glanced to my side and I swear I saw Ull blush.

"I do not know how or why The Fates have brought you to our family, but I am very grateful that you would choose to give up your parents, your friends, the only world you have ever known . . . for us. Thank you for choosing my son." Sif embraced me warmly, surprising me with the sincerity of her emotion. Thor nodded from some feet away. I knew he wasn't an emotional man and that small gesture spoke volumes.

I pulled back. "Thank you for sharing Ull with me. And thank you for giving us your blessing. I love him more than I will ever be able to explain."

"I know." Her simple reply was offset by her dazzling smile.

"Shall we eat before we go?" Thor spoke from the table. "These things tend to take a while."

He should know. Apparently he'd been to twenty of them.

"Yes. Kristia? Mother?" Ull stood and held out an arm. We filled our plates and dug in.

Gunnar and Inga opened the front door just as we were finishing.

"How was the shooting range?" Ull called as they darted toward their bedroom.

"Great!" Inga's hair flew behind her as she tore out of the room. Two minutes later she emerged wearing a graduation robe. Her hair shone like she'd just brushed it, and she was artfully applying mascara in the middle of the living room. She didn't even need a mirror.

"How do you *do* that?" I asked.

"Centuries of practice. You'll get the hang of it."

Gunnar strolled behind Inga, also wearing his graduation outfit. "Look." He pointed to his sleeve. "Mine has those fuzzy things on it this time."

"Smarty pants." Inga stood on tiptoes to kiss his jaw. "Now let's go. We don't want to be late."

Our peculiar little party walked the few blocks to campus. When we reached the field where the graduation was being held, we heard a spry voice.

"Kristia, Ull!" Elsker was waving from a row of seats. "Over here."

"Oh, good. Second row. I hate when we can't see you turn your tassel." Sif patted her son's back.

"Ull, can I borrow you?" Elsker whisked Ull a few feet away. They had a hushed conversation, before Ull walked back to me with a frown.

"What was that about?" I whispered.

"Nothing." He forced a smile and kissed my cheek.

"Uh-uh, that's not going to work this time. Was it about Ragnarok?"

"No, darling." He opened my hand and kissed my palm, staring into my eyes as he pulled his lips away. "Everything is fine."

"Ull!"

"You had better take a seat." Ull waved at Olaug, who now sat next to Elsker. "The ceremony is about to begin."

"You know I'll get it out of you eventually."

"I have no doubt you will." He smiled.

But for the next hour, speeches, congratulations, and the official handing out of diplomas commanded my attention. By the time Ull turned his tassel from one side of his hat to the other, I'd almost forgotten the conversation with Elsker. And between Sif's tears and Elsker's monologue on the importance of a good education, I didn't have a chance to follow up.

"Are you okay?" Ull whispered as Elsker went on about the value of Midgard's university system.

"It's bittersweet, isn't it? The end of the year?" I twined my fingers through his and held tight.

"A bit." We scanned the thinning crowd, looking at the sea of faces we'd come to recognize over the last year.

"I know we're keeping our options open about next year, but if I don't re-enroll, this is kind of it, isn't it? For being in Cardiff, I mean." My eyes darted from the tree where Ull had first asked me for my notes, to the field where we'd read our textbooks on the rare warm afternoons, before resting on the cafeteria where we shared lunch most days.

"I would imagine so." Ull smiled down at me. "But that is a good thing. We have new adventures awaiting us."

He tilted his head. In the distance I could see the steeple of the Norse church where Ull had taken me so many months ago, in what I saw now as the beginning of my life. And where, in just a few days' time, we would become husband and wife. He squeezed my hand, lost in the same thoughts I was. It had been quite a year.

❄❄❄❄

"You're sure you've got your honeymoon wardrobe sorted?" The next afternoon, Inga stood in her living room with her hands on her hips. She'd been going over some wedding details with me, and she seemed genuinely surprised when I told her the only thing I had left to do was buy sunscreen for our mystery destination. I had no idea if immortal me would burn as badly as regular me, and I still didn't know if we'd be honeymooning in a summery climate, but it seemed prudent to be prepared for all scenarios.

"I've had my sundries packed for two weeks. And Victoria took care of most of the actual clothes." I closed my notebook and put it in my bag. "Ull still won't tell me where we're going, but he knows Victoria's been designing some dresses for me to wear. He told her just enough that she volunteered to pack for me."

"You, Miss Planner, are letting someone *else* pack for you?" Inga raised an eyebrow. "How's that going over?"

"It's driving me nuts," I admitted. "But I gave Victoria two lists—one for a warm, and one for a cold-weather destination. I'm trusting she'll follow my suggestions."

"Yeah, because that Victoria is a real list follower when it comes to clothes." Inga snickered. "I wouldn't worry, Kristia. I'm sure whatever she packs for you will be absolutely fabulous."

"That's what I'm afraid of," I muttered. I really hoped Victoria packed at least one pair of comfortable shoes. High fashion wasn't exactly easy to walk in.

"Well, then I guess the only place we need to go today is the drugstore. What kind of sunscreen do you wear?" Inga picked up her purse and walked toward the door. I grabbed my bag and followed.

"SPF 55. Should we close the windows before we lock up the . . ." I trailed off as the sound of a grating female voice came from outside. "Who is that?"

Inga held her finger to her lips. We tiptoed to the window and peeked around the curtain. Ull had just gotten home, and was getting out of his Range Rover. He walked around the front of the car and stood on the sidewalk, wearing a thin, black sweater and blue jeans. He folded his arms across his chest and stared unhappily at the female rushing toward him, screeching his name.

"Hi Ull." The woman waggled her fingers. She wore tight jeans, sky-high heels, and a top that once again failed to cover her substantial assets. She tossed her chocolaty-brown hair over her shoulder as she sauntered up the sidewalk. When I recognized whom she was, my stomach clenched in a tight ball. Ull took a step backward, his substantial form blocking the path to the front door.

"Stop right there, Skadi," he ordered. His voice carried through the open window.

Skadi stuck out her lower lip, then pushed her chest out for good measure. "Is that any way to treat a friend?"

"She's not his friend," Inga muttered beside me.

"Shh," I hissed. I didn't want Skadi to look up and see us spying on her.

Down on the sidewalk, Ull didn't budge. "What do you want?"

"I came to see your dad." Skadi lifted her chin.

"You came all the way to Midgard to see Thor?"

"Yes." Skadi smiled.

Inga's shoulders were so tense, they were practically shaking. "Did she . . . that cow bleached her teeth. What the Helheim is she trying to pull?"

I ran my tongue over the tops of my own teeth. Three brushings a day, and they were pearly white. "Ull isn't going to let her inside, is he?" I asked.

"Does he look like he's budging?" Inga pointed out.

Ull had adjusted his stance so his feet were shoulder-width apart. With his crossed arms, he now fully blocked the walkway to our door.

"No," I acquiesced.

Outside, Ull stared Skadi down. "My father is not here right now. And he is not interested in seeing you. We heard about your little stunt with Kristia, and we are not amused."

"What stunt?" Flinging a hand to her mouth, Skadi made herself the picture of virtue. "I was only trying to welcome Kristia to Asgard. Did the human get herself upset?"

"Drop the act. Why are you really here?" Ull's voice was cool as he picked a piece of lint off his sweater. I couldn't help but admire his calm. Pressure suited Ull.

Skadi kept her chest out and shifted her weight to one leg, so her hip jutted out. Ardis used that move—she said it was guaranteed to showcase curves to their maximum advantage. The back of my neck broke out in a sweat as I stared at the goddess, batting her eyes like she was trying to start a sandstorm. There was no denying that Skadi was hitting on my man.

Beside me, Inga sounded every bit as angry as I felt. "So help me, if she pushes her ta-tas any closer to his face, I will go out there myself and gauge her eyes out."

"You and me both," I muttered. But I couldn't take my eyes off the scene on the sidewalk.

"What are you doing with the mortal, Ull? You know I can give you so much more than she can." Skadi stepped closer to my betrothed and touched his arm. "We're *equals*. I could take care of you in ways she'll never be able to."

My stomach churned. Of all the underhanded, unethical . . . *common* things to do. My pulse thundered in my ears. I was about to see red.

"Wait for it," Inga murmured. She reached over to hold my hand. "Captain Overprotective is about to suit up. This is gonna be epic."

Sure enough, Ull jerked away from Skadi's touch. He leaned forward so his face was inches from hers, and let out a growl. "I do not know what game you are playing, but I do not want you to come near my fiancée again. She is about to become my *wife*, and I will not allow anyone, especially a half-crazed lunatic, to hurt her. We know what you did to Njord after he broke up with you. It took three healers four full hours to set him right. Do you really think I would leave the sweetest girl I have ever met for someone who would do *that*?"

Skadi blinked. "I don't know what you're talking about."

"Give it up, Skadi. Jens told me everything. If you know what is good for you, you will stay away from my girl. Because if you do not, so help me Odin, I will have you shipped off to the icy wasteland or the fiery inferno. Your choice."

Skadi's eyes sparked with anger. "You're being stupid, Ull. You'll never be happy with her."

"Goodbye, Skadi." Ull leaned back, and hooked his thumbs in the pockets of his jeans. "I will be sure to tell my father you stopped by."

Skadi gave Ull a furious glare and stormed down the street. The knot in my stomach unraveled as Ull spun on one heel and walked the short distance to the front door. He turned the knob and pushed through, pausing when he noticed Inga and I standing at the window.

"You saw all that," he surmised.

I nodded.

"You okay?" He eyed me carefully.

I ran across the room and threw my arms around his neck. Ull stumbled back, caught off-guard.

"Sweetheart?"

I pulled my head back to look into his eyes. "You sent her packing."

"Of course I did. You are my girl."

"I love you," I whispered.

"I love you too," Ull said. He lowered his mouth onto mine, and gave me a soft kiss. "*Now* do you believe I want *nothing* to do with Skadi?"

I gazed up at him adoringly. "I do."

"That wench is a rotten troll," Inga chimed in from the window. "I wanted to come out there and send her back to the rock she crawled out from under."

"Where *did* she come from?" I turned to Ull. "Inga said she's not really one of you guys."

"I have my theories," Ull muttered. "But I would rather not talk about Skadi anymore." He glanced at the bags slung over our shoulders. "Were you two going somewhere?"

"To the drugstore. I figure I'll need sunscreen for wherever you're taking me, right? Sun *or* snow?" I reached up to stroke the stubble along his jaw.

"You will get no hints from me, woman." Ull smiled. "But if it is not a girls-only trip, I will join you. I need to pick up a few last-minute items myself."

"Anything in particular? If it's something you've never purchased before, I'm sure Gunnar would be happy to tag along and offer some advice." Inga fluttered her lashes as Ull shot her a glare.

"Bug off." Ull opened the front door and held out his hand for me. "After you, my lady." As an afterthought he added, "and Inga."

Inga stuck out her tongue, then followed me outside. Ull locked the front door and laced his fingers through mine. I gave his hand a squeeze and rested my head on his shoulder as we walked the few blocks to the shop.

Ull leaned down and brushed his lips against my hair. "You happy?"

"Tremendously." I sighed. Our wedding was days away. We were about to embark on our honeymoon. And the love of my life had just shut down an honest-to-goodness goddess because he wanted to be with *me*. Happy didn't begin to cover the way I felt.

It was a feeling I wanted to hold on to forever.

❄❄❄❄

Ull and I were at the station on Wednesday night when Ardis's train pulled in. She hopped off onto the platform, chestnut hair shining in a chic bob that peeked from beneath her pageboy cap. Her eyes searched the station before they came to rest on Ull. She lowered her gaze to confirm he was with me, and when I waved, her eyes grew big as saucers.

"Get out," she mouthed.

I giggled.

"Kristia!" She ran to us and threw her arms around me. Ull pretended not to hear when she whispered, "Good God, he is hot."

I untangled myself and grinned. "Ardis, this is Ull,

my fiancé. Ull, this is my best friend from Nehalem, Ardis."

"It is a pleasure to meet you, Ardis." Ull's words were lost on my friend. She couldn't seem to find her voice under his penetrating gaze. I knew the feeling all too well. Watching Ardis weakly shake his hand, I marveled at how far I'd come in a year.

Thankfully, Ull drove us straight to my flat and headed home. I don't think Ardis could have kept it together beyond the time it took to get to my place. She stood in my doorway, mouth still slightly open, while Ull deposited her suitcase at the step and leaned down to kiss me goodnight.

"The next time I see you, you will be Mrs. Myhr." He gave me a look that left *me* barely holding it together.

I kissed him dreamily, stretching on my tiptoes to wrap my arms around his neck. He kissed me back with such intensity, I forgot about our audience. His lips moved against mine, and I grabbed at his hair, wrapping the strands around my fingers. I breathed in his woodsy scent, dizzy at the sensation of his hands stroking the small of my back. In the morning I would be his wife—I couldn't believe this was happening.

Ull released himself from my embrace with a throaty groan. "*God natt,* darling. Ardis." He nodded at my girlfriend, then walked briskly to the Range Rover, glancing back once to give me a wink.

He'd driven to the end of the block and turned the corner before either Ardis or I could find our voices. She was the first to speak. "You lucky wench."

I laughed, both with relief at seeing her again and nerves at the enormity of the week ahead. She joined me in my laughter and we headed into the tiny flat. Emma and Victoria looked up from the program they'd been watching, expectant smiles on their faces.

"You must be Ardis." Emma jumped up to hug my friend. "It's nice to have you here. Kristia has been so excited that you were coming."

Victoria stood, holding out her hand. "It's nice to meet you," she said, more reserved than Emma. She raised one perfectly arched eyebrow. "So did you meet *him*?"

"Oh. My. God." It was all Ardis had to say. The ice was broken and Emma pulled her toward the couch.

"He's totally gorgeous, isn't he?" Emma's enthusiasm bubbled over.

"Our girl chose very well," Victoria agreed with a wink. "Of course, so did Ull."

I batted my eyes at Victoria. "Well bless your heart."

"I cannot believe you get to marry *that*. That," Ardis continued with authority, "is without a doubt the most beautiful man I have *ever* seen. Ever." She emphasized.

"I know! The face! The arms! The body . . ." Victoria waggled her eyebrows and I blushed.

This conversation had veered way off course. "Enough about Ull's body. How was your cast party? You didn't have to leave early to make your flight, did you?" I asked Ardis.

"Oh, Lord no. I stayed until four a.m. It totally

rocked!"

"Tell us about it," Emma probed.

"We had it at this super trendy bar around the corner from the theatre. There was this amazing DJ from LA, and half the theatre school turned out. Plus like, a dozen celebrities showed up. Mostly reality stars, but still. We went for pizza after, and just walked around the city until dawn. Then I booked it for the airport."

"God, it sounds amazing." Victoria exhaled. "I would love to see New York someday."

"Well there's always Fashion Week," Emma reminded her. Turning to Ardis she explained, "Victoria's taken a job with Alexander McQueen after graduation. She's going to be a famous designer!"

"I'm going to be a lowly assistant," Victoria corrected. "But then a famous designer."

"Wow, that's awesome." Ardis was impressed.

"It will be an adventure," Victoria said with uncharacteristic modesty. "And Emma is going to stay on at Cardiff to earn her Master's."

"Maybe I can land a hot grad student like Kristia did." Emma giggled.

"If it were that easy, I'd sign up for grad school, too." Ardis chuckled. I sat back happily, watching my dearest girlfriend interact with the two women who had seen me through the biggest year of my life. Everything was as it should be. My friends were here to celebrate with me, and tomorrow I would embark on a destiny I had never seen coming. At this moment in time, my life was absolutely perfect.

CHAPTER ELEVEN

***"I LIKE YOUR FRIEND,"** a raspy voice hissed from the end of my bed.*

"Hmm." I rolled over and pulled the covers up to my ears.

"The one sleeping on the couch. She seems very nice."

"Uhhhh." I pulled a pillow over my head for good measure.

"It would be a shame if anything were to happen to her."

I snapped to attention. I knew that voice. Oh, come on. Elf Man had to show up the night before my wedding?

"Please, for the love of all that is good, go away. This is not the best night for me."

"I could just leave, sweet Kristia. But then I wouldn't be able to give you the terrible news."

"What news?" I sat up reluctantly and tucked the comforter under my arms, wishing I'd worn more than a

sheer camisole top to bed.

"Something horrible happened to your beloved Olaug."

"So help me, if you've done anything to hurt her—"

"Oh, it wasn't me." The evil creature broke into an ear-splitting grin. "She has fallen ill. Of natural causes."

I eyed him levelly. "What did you do?"

"I may have opened the gateway, but the disease found her all on its own."

"Bull. Fix this."

"Oh, but I can't." He feigned disappointment. "This is a powerful disease. A magical disease. It would have to be. After all, gods don't get sick."

"So how did Olaug get this magical disease then?"

The elf raised his shoulders. "Now what kind of a challenge would this be if I told you that?"

"You tell me how to make her better, or I swear on my grandmother's grave, I will spend every minute of the rest of my life hunting down your sorry behind. And when I find you—"

"Ooh, such threats from a human. But you don't scare me. And to prove it, I'll throw you a bone. The only way to heal your precious Olaug is to destroy me."

"My pleasure." I grabbed for my necklace, knowing it had nearly killed him twice before. I was more than ready to finish the job. But my fist closed on nothing. My throat was bare. Frantically, I dug around in the sheets. It had to have fallen—I never took it off. But after a moment, I remembered the necklace was resting in a solvent in the bathroom. I'd left it to soak overnight so it would shine for the wedding. It was a treasure of

Asgard, after all, and it deserved its moment in the sun.

"Missing something?" Elf Man fingered his neck idly, mocking me. I stood, dropping the comforter and moving toward the door. "Oh, Kristia. I'm afraid I can't let you do that. I have to kill you."

"In your dreams." I ran for the door, but he grabbed my arm before I was halfway there. I swung, putting all my weight behind my fist, but the gesture was futile. Elfie blocked it with an easy parry and landed a punch of his own in my gut. I doubled over, gasping for breath. Ull was going to have to make good on his promise to train me if he expected me to survive Ragnarok.

"Oh, poppet. Did I hurt you?" The demon kicked me in the thigh, forcing me to the floor. My vision blurred and I could barely make out his legs as he walked toward me. He lifted his hands over my torso and started to mutter an incantation. I had no idea what it meant, but I knew it wasn't going to end well for me. My brain got very fuzzy and I realized I was losing consciousness. At the same time a sharp pain was forming in my chest—something was literally squeezing the life out of me.

I had to act fast if I was going to live. Using my last bit of strength, I grabbed the leg right in front of my face and bit down on the monster's Achilles' tendon. Hard.

He let out a high pitched shriek and I took another bite. The thud must have meant he'd fallen over, and as soon as the incantation stopped, my consciousness flickered back into focus.

I didn't have any time to lose. Without sparing a

thought for the ache in my gut, I pushed myself to my feet and bolted. I ran for the door and down the short hallway until I reached the bathroom. My necklace was right where I'd left it. I grabbed it with a tight fist and it erupted, beams of light shooting from between my firmly clenched fingers. The elf was right behind me. He dropped to the floor as soon as the lights appeared. They pierced his body, my saving swords, and he writhed in pain as the beams sliced through his flesh again and again. After a short eternity, he vanished with a pop.

My hands trembled as I fastened the clasp around my neck, and I made my way down the hall on shaky legs. Ardis was snoring on the couch where I'd left her, and Emma and Victoria's doors were still closed. How had they slept through that?

I rubbed at my bruised leg as I limped back to my room. Sleep was the furthest thing from my mind. Should I wake up Ull? He'd ordered me to call him immediately if I ever saw Elf Man again. Of course, he'd also ordered me to keep my necklace on at all times. Oops.

No matter, I knew Ull would be beyond furious if I didn't call. He wouldn't care that I'd done a halfway-decent job of taking care of things on my own. I shuffled to my bed and found my phone on my nightstand. At least one thing was where it was supposed to be tonight.

"Darling." Ull sounded groggy. "Are you having wedding jitters?"

"No, I'm fine." It was such a relief to hear his voice.

I was more shaken than I wanted to admit. "But you have to check on Olaug. Can you reach her?"

"I am not calling my grandmother at three in the morning."

"Ull, she's sick. Or she's going to be. We were wrong—Elfie isn't after me. He's after Olaug."

"What are you talking about?" Ull sounded more alert. "She cannot get sick."

"I know that. The elf did it, he cast some kind of spell or something, and she's going to get some magic disease. The only way to make her better is to destroy him, but I tried and even though he disappeared I don't think he's really gone."

"Kristia Tostenson, when did he show up again?"

"Just now. He was in my room when I woke up."

"And did you use your necklace right away like I told you?"

"About that." I chewed on my lip. "It was sort of in another room. I was cleaning it overnight—you know, for the wedding."

"Sweetheart!" Ull's frustration rang through the phone.

"Well, it was dirty! I couldn't very well get married wearing a dirty necklace, now, could I? Besides, I got to it in time. It did the whole light-shooting thing again and it looked like it sliced him up pretty good. But then he just disappeared. I don't know where he went."

"Did he hurt you?"

"A little," I admitted. "But I'm okay. Really."

"That is it. I am coming over there." I could hear

the rustling of clothes.

"No!" I panicked. "It's bad luck for us to see each other the night before our wedding."

"Do you really think I am concerned with a mortal superstition at a time like this?"

"You should be. Divorce rates are high these days, and considering the odds are stacked fairly well against us to begin with—"

"Sweetheart." I could hear Ull's smile through the phone. "Except in very extreme circumstances, Asgardians do not divorce. We mate for life. And since you will become one of us tomorrow, it is not something you will need to worry about either. I am coming over."

"Well, I'm still a human today. Tonight. Whatever. And I'm sticking to this. You can't see me until we're at the church. Period."

Ull sighed. "I need to know that you are all right.

"I'm fine. Honest." A little shaken up. Maybe a little bruised. But nothing a good night's sleep with my necklace firmly in its rightful place wouldn't fix.

"I do not believe you."

"Remember, you promised to start trusting me."

"Touché, Miss Tostenson. Or may I call you Mrs. Myhr?"

"Not for another couple of hours." My brain was too tired to do the math. "But I would feel better if you checked on Olaug."

"I will call you back in five minutes." With that he hung up.

Precisely four minutes later my mobile rang. "Is

she okay?" I answered breathlessly.

"She was. Until I called and woke her up. Now she is mad at me."

"Sorry. But isn't she sick?"

"No. She had no idea what I was talking about, either. She said nobody had cast any spells on her. She is the pinnacle of physical health, thanks in large part to a strict regimen of, her words now, *good food, brisk walks, and regular sleep*."

"Oh." I was stumped. "Then what did the elf mean?"

"He was probably just trying to get into your head."

"Maybe." That didn't make sense. Why would he want to play mind games before he tried to kill me?

"Are you sure you do not want me to come over?"

"Positive."

"Are you wearing your necklace now?"

The threat was clear. If I answered wrong, I knew I'd have a large Adonis on my doorstep. "Yes."

"Good girl. Try to get some sleep. You have a big day tomorrow."

"You can be really bossy, you know that?"

"I do. But it is for your own good."

"In your dreams." I laughed.

"I shall see you at the church." Ull's voice sounded husky.

"I can't wait," I whispered. For a lot of reasons, morning couldn't come fast enough.

CHAPTER TWELVE

THURSDAY, THOR'S DAY TO the Norse party, dawned foggy and cool. It was just like so many of my days in Cardiff, and I couldn't imagine it any other way. How was it already time to say goodbye to this place? Cardiff was where my life truly began; it was where I fell in love with Ull. And now we could be together forever—literally.

But first, there was one teensy detail to take care of.

"Are you ready?" Inga asked when she picked me up. She wore a hot-pink terry sweat-suit and pale-pink Uggs, and her hair was pulled up in a messy bun. "Why are you looking at me like that?"

"I'm just not used to casual Inga. I like it." I placed the large garment bag across the back seat. The dress was our cover for our morning outing. We'd told my friends we were going to have it taken in one final time before the wedding. In actuality, we were doing an adjustment of an entirely different nature. I fastened my seatbelt and Inga started her car.

"It's early," she huffed. "And I used all my energy kicking the boys out of the house this morning. Ull did *not* want to miss being there for your transformation prep. I told him we were just doing superficial girly stuff to get you ready for the wedding—hair, and nails, and waxing, you know? But he was still worried about you. Made me promise to call him if you seemed even the slightest bit stressed out about being changed. I practically had to wrestle him into Gunnar's car. I didn't have any time left for fashion."

"Please. You look amazing. You always do."

"Oh." Inga adjusted her rear-view mirror as she sped through the streets of Cardiff. "Thank you."

"Welcome." I fiddled with the wrists of my sweater.

"How are you feeling?"

"Terrified."

"You don't have to go through with this." She shot me a sideways look.

"I want to go through with it," I insisted. "I love Ull more than anything, and I want to be with him for a hundred lifetimes. But that doesn't make crossing over any less scary. Are you sure it's not going to hurt?"

"Well . . ." Inga nibbled on her bottom lip; something else I'd never seen her do.

"Oh my gosh. You guys aren't sure! That's why you made Ull leave!"

"We're not a hundred percent sure," Inga admitted. "I mean, we've never exactly done it before. But we don't *think* it'll hurt. Why should it hurt? It's just a transference of matter, and a mutation of brain cells that—"

"You're doing what to my brain cells? Olaug didn't say anything about that." I pulled so hard at my sweater that I heard a small rip.

"Relax." Inga rolled her eyes and steered swiftly into a space in front of her flat. "It's going to be super easy. *We think*," she muttered under her breath.

"I heard that." I shoved my thumb through the new hole in my sweater and made a fist.

"Don't be a weenie. Come on." She marched toward the house. I followed behind, wobbling like the seniors in Mormor's bridge club after one too many egg-salad sandwiches. I was suddenly super queasy.

"*Hei hei*, Kristia," Olaug greeted me from inside. "Happy wedding day."

My anxiety ebbed. Whatever else happened, this day would end with a wedding.

"I get to marry him today." I looked at Olaug's shining eyes.

"You get to marry him today." She beamed back at me. "Let's just do one little thing first."

"You lied to me. It's going to hurt."

"I won't let it." She took my hand and walked me down the hall. Ull's bedroom had been set up like a laboratory. Heavy white tapestries hung over the windows and his furniture was pushed to the walls. A stainless steel table stood in the corner, holding a range of tubes, vials, and three disconcertingly large needles. In the center of the room stood one high-backed chair with straps on the armrests.

I felt lost as last year's Easter egg.

"You've got to be kidding me," I muttered. My eyes were locked on the restraint-laden chair.

"It's just a precaution," Inga pleaded. "We don't know what to expect."

I took a deep breath. "Right."

"You don't have to do it, Kristia." Olaug stood directly in front of me, shaking her head.

"Yes, I do." I squeezed my eyes shut and pictured standing at the altar with Ull. I wanted to go through with this—for us. "It's just . . ."

"I know." She squeezed my arm and helped me into the chair.

"So what happens now?" I closed my eyes as Olaug snapped the arm restraints into place.

"Idunn will prep you." Inga came up behind me and put her hands on my shoulders.

"Idunn, Goddess of Wisdom, Idunn?" My eyes flew open.

"One and the same." An absolute vision walked into the room. The woman was dressed head-to-toe in white, with thick brown hair and piercing blue eyes. She crossed to the steel table and put on a pair of surgical gloves. "Sorry I'm late, I was just washing up."

"*Hei,*" Olaug greeted at the goddess.

Inga nodded nervously. "Hey."

"Morning," I croaked.

"Ladies," Idunn responded with a smile. She picked up one of the vials and came to stand beside me. After pouring the liquid onto a cotton ball, she dabbed at my temples. I sucked in a sharp breath. *That burned.*

"It's okay. The stinging will pass quickly." Idunn was right. She crossed back to the table and swapped the vial for another, repeating the procedure on my throat and wrists. She moved with the assurance of someone who'd done this a hundred times before, though of course that couldn't be.

"So, you work as a surgeon?" I asked hopefully.

"No. We don't have surgeons in Asgard. We never get sick." Idunn swiped one last cotton ball between my eyes and patted my hand. "But I am the realm's most gifted horticulturist. I develop the apple hybrids that foster our eternal youth."

So Asgard's top plant doctor was about to operate on my brain. Brilliant.

"I also trained at Harvard's medical school a few years back at Odin's insistence. He takes the Ragnarok prophecy very seriously, and wants to make sure we're prepared for all eventualities. My specialty was neurosurgery."

Well that made me feel a little bit better.

"Relax, Kristia. This will be over before you know it." Idunn picked up one of the needles and drew out the contents of one of the tubes.

"Right."

"Would it help if I explained the procedure to you?" she asked.

"Sure." Not that it mattered, one way or the other. I was absolutely going through with this—an eternity with Ull was worth anything the good doctor could throw at me. But I shot an accusatory glance at Olaug.

She'd left out some key bits. Like my brain being injected with giant needles.

"In layman's terms, I'm going to take some of the matter out of your brain and replace it with cells from Inga's cerebellum."

"That's the part that's responsible for my lack of grace, right?" I stared at Idunn.

"It's the region that oversees motor control." Idunn nodded.

"So if I'm getting some of Inga's motor skills . . . wait, you donated brain cells for me?" I turned to Inga.

She shrugged. "What are friends for?"

Idunn stood in front of me. "After I inject the cells, I'll transfer nine units of gardium into your hypothalamus. That's the 'god gene' we've been developing for you."

"The god gene," I mused. A genetic Higgs-boson.

"Yes. And it will sit dormant until Odin activates it. That's the second part of the process. I do the science, he does the magic. When Odin calls on Mjölnir, it'll be like a car getting a jump-start. The synapses will connect and your immortal existence will begin."

"When will my . . . uh, mortal existence end?" I asked.

"When I remove the matter from your brain. The transference of Inga's cells for yours will be quick, but for that brief moment you will technically be brain-dead." Idunn spoke matter-of-factly.

"Oh."

"Don't worry, Kristia. I performed over a hundred brain surgeries during my time as a neurosurgeon.

And I never lost a patient."

"But did you ever deliberately kill one to make her immortal?"

"Well, no," Idunn admitted. "But no matter. I'm not going to tarnish a perfect record."

"Wait. When you . . . take stuff out of my brain . . . is there any chance I could lose my visions?" A lot was riding on my being able to see stuff after I was changed. Important stuff. Like how to save the cosmos as we knew it.

"Oh, not at all. I will be removing matter from your cerebellum. Your visions operate from another region of your brain," Idunn explained.

"Oh." I wanted to ask more, but my throat went dry when Idunn approached with the enormous needle.

"Let's get started." She raised the syringe.

"Are you going to knock me out first?" I bleated.

"It's better if I don't. I need a clear scan on your brain waves, and that's going to be tough if you're unconscious." Idunn blinked.

I grabbed Inga's arm and pulled so her ear was level with my mouth. "If I don't make it, tell Ull I loved him."

"Stop it," she hissed. But I could see the fear in her eyes.

"How'd you get Ull to agree to this?" I whispered.

"I told you. He has no idea what we're doing," Inga admitted. "He thinks your 'prep' involves an intense beauty ritual. Exfoliating and stuff."

"So he doesn't know about the . . ." My eyes shifted

to the table full of needles and tubes.

"No." She shook her head. "He'd never have agreed to let it happen. Should I have told him?"

I thought about it. On the one hand, I'd pledged complete honesty in everything I did. Ull wanted what was best for me, and if he would have stopped this from happening maybe it was too risky after all. But on the other hand, this was the only way Ull and I had a shot at surviving Ragnarok. If I stayed human, my visions would be useless to the gods and we'd all be goners anyway. No matter how scary it was, this had to happen.

"No. You were right not to tell him. But you know he's going to be furious if he ever finds out." I lay my head against the back of the chair, imagining Ull's overreaction to the news that I'd let some goddess I'd never met inject me with Inga's brain cells. "Listen, I'm going to be brain-dead. And I know that's not a huge deal when you're immortal, but I'm not there yet. And on the off chance Idunn slips—"

"I've never slipped." Idunn wagged her finger.

"Okay, on the off chance I don't, uh, make it through this thing, I want you to tell Ull . . ." I trailed off. There was so much I wanted Ull to know. How much I loved him. How my life was completely meaningless before he came into it. How I felt more alive now than I had in nineteen years, even though there was a very strong possibility I'd face death by one means or another in the next three months.

"You'll be fine," Inga swore.

"Right. But just in case. Tell him he's my world.

And no matter how it pans out, it was all worth it." I squeezed Inga's hand.

"I'll tell him." She squeezed me back. "Just get through this, okay?"

I nodded. "I'm ready."

Inga moved to my left side, holding tight to my fingers. "I'll be here the whole time," she pledged.

"I will, too." Olaug came up to grasp my right hand. "Bring her over safely, Idunn."

"I plan to." The doctor stood directly in front of me, the oversized needle in hand ready to siphon out my mortality. "Now close your eyes, Kristia. And *do not move*."

I stared at the bookcase directly in front of me. Ull had given my Christmas gift a place of honor on the top shelf. I'd stood outside the Millennium Stadium locker room until every member of the national team signed that rugby ball for him, and he called it the most thoughtful gift he'd ever received. Until today. Knowing that I would give up my human life for him was a gift he said he'd never be able to repay, but he'd spend the rest of his existence showing me how much it meant to him.

Only he had it all backwards. *I* would never be able to repay *him* for letting me be a part of his life. For loving me beyond the bounds of logic, and letting me feel a joy, security, and belonging I hadn't even known existed.

Ull. I was doing this for Ull. And no matter how scary it was to know I was about to be brain-dead, it was something I'd do a hundred times over if it meant even one extra day with him.

I squeezed my eyes shut and made fists around Olaug and Inga's fingers. My grip was so tight my knuckles burned, and when the needle pierced my skin I fought every impulse and stayed still. The metal pushed through my flesh, pausing as it touched my skull. I heard Idunn murmur an incantation in Norwegian, and the needle moved through the bone, sending white-hot pain in all directions. My forehead felt like it was on fire, the searing pulses a thousand times more intense than even the worst vision-induced headache. Idunn continued her chant, repeating the same nine words over and over as the needle burrowed deeper in my skull. The slow movement was excruciating, and I hoped when it finally broke through the bone the agony might end.

I must have forgotten what was on the other side.

When the needle cleared the skull it hit my brain. Idunn began a new chant as the object pushed into the soft matter. Mind-numbing anguish shot directly through every nerve in my body. I forgot everything the doctor told me and bucked against the needle. I felt it probing the corners of my head, stabbing the soft matter as I moved. But I couldn't stop.

"She's seizing!" I heard Inga's voice but I couldn't register anything else. My body convulsed wildly, fighting against the chair's restraints as I tried desperately to expel the needle from my brain.

"Hold her down." The edge in Idunn's voice would have worried me if I'd been able to think of anything but getting that thing *out*.

"I'm trying!"

I fought against the pressure, wrenching and pulling, anything to be free of the object searing my brain, but my arms were trapped. A heavy weight against my chest stopped the bucking. Only the pain remained.

"That's it." I felt Idunn's cool hand on my forehead as she pushed me against the chair. I let out a moan. The cold was a welcome respite.

"Steady." The burning resumed as the needle found its path again, this time pushing straight into the center of my head. I tried to focus on the image of Ull standing at the altar of the church; pledging his life to me; kissing me for the first time as my husband. I tried to remember the reason I was doing this. But the injection moved deeper and I exploded from the inside, a thousand fissures erupting from the mutinous metal invading my mind. Each fissure felt like a stake driving through the hypersensitive nerve endings in what was left of my mind.

Then the pain changed. Instead of an outward heat I felt an unbearable suctioning. Now my head was imploding. The entire mass of my brain felt like it was being sucked through an impossibly tiny straw. The pressure was unbearable, and I spiraled down an endless tunnel of torture. Just when I thought I couldn't take it anymore I felt the needle pull out of my brain, back though the skull, and out of my skin.

And then everything was dark.

CHAPTER THIRTEEN

WHEN I OPENED MY eyes, Olaug knelt in front of me.

"Stay very still, Kristia. I do not want you to over exert yourself. Blink once if you can hear me." She stared into my eyes.

I blinked.

"Good. Now I am going to ask you a few questions. Do not answer if it's too painful. Are you ready?"

I blinked again.

"Okay. What is my name?" She stared into my eyes.

I stared back.

"What's my name?" she repeated.

"Olaug."

"Good. Where am I from?"

"Why—"

"Just answer me. Where am I from?"

"You're from Asgard," I answered.

"And what are you going to do today?"

I wracked my brain. Where was I? I glanced at my arms, tied down to a white chair. I looked to my left and saw Inga, holding my hand. To my right, Idunn stood next to a table of medical equipment. She stared at me as she wrung her hands together. I glanced at the needles on the table and everything came rushing back to me. The searing pain. The vacuous pressure. The darkness.

"Kristia, you must focus. What are you going to do today?" Olaug repeated.

I sifted through the fog of confusion until I found my footing. A soft smile played at the corner of my mouth. "I'm marrying my best friend."

"That's my girl." Olaug's shoulders dropped, a visible sign of her relief. Inga let out a quiet sigh, and Idunn closed her eyes and tilted her head to the ceiling. "You're going to be all right."

Inga undid my restraints, and leaned in for a gentle hug. "Thank Odin you're okay. That was scary."

"It felt scary." I'd been sure I was dying. I rubbed at my wrists and tried not to think.

"I am sorry, Kristia." Idunn shook her head. "I should have sedated you."

"Yeah, that would have been nice." My head still felt like the byproduct of the mortar and pestle Mormor used to whip up her guacamole. "But I'm good now. You got what you needed?"

"I did," Idunn affirmed.

"So I'm ready for Odin?"

"You're ready."

"Then let's do this." I tried to stand and fell back. "Whoa."

Idunn handed me a cup of juice. "You went

through a *lot* this morning. Don't push yourself too hard just yet."

"Okay," I drained the cup and closed my eyes. I gingerly touched my temples. "When will the pounding stop?"

"We don't really know. I'm so sorry, Kristia. Here, come lie down." Inga helped me up and moved me to Ull's bed. It was so soft; the thick pillows pulled me into their depths. Inga tucked a heavy blanket over me.

"I can't sleep," I protested despite my brain's obvious willingness. "I have to get ready for the church."

"Shh." Inga stroked my hair. "We're way ahead of schedule. We don't have to be back to your flat for another two hours."

"But my friends—" My words started to slur. I was a heartbeat away from the deepest rest I'd ever known.

"They think we're at the seamstress with your dress, remember? Brides always lose a few extra pounds in that last week." Inga's gentle voice was the last push I needed. I closed my eyes and gave in to the overwhelming need to sleep.

❄ ❄ ❄ ❄

When I came to, Ull's bedroom was back to normal. Inga and Olaug had rearranged the furniture while I slept, and I'd been so out of it, I'd slept right through them moving the bed. The medical equipment was nowhere to be seen, and the throbbing in my head had stilled to a barely-there ache. For a brief moment I wondered if I'd dreamed the whole thing.

"Well hello, Sleeping Beauty." Inga grinned from the foot of the bed. "She's up, Idunn."

The white-clad woman came to my side, slapped a blood pressure cuff on my arm and held out a thermometer. I opened my mouth obediently, and waited for the beep.

"Your vitals are fine." Idunn smiled. "You are cleared of my care. Now talk to Elsker and then go get ready for your wedding. I'll see you at the church."

"Wait, Elsker's here?" I sat up slowly, and touched my head. The ache was subsiding.

"She is. And I need to leave to go find Odin so we can go over his part of your change-over." Idunn leaned over and squeezed me softly. "Take care of our Ull. He deserves this happiness."

"I will." I hugged her back. "And thank you. For everything."

"Are you ready, Kristia?" Elsker came into the room and sat on the bed next to me.

"I didn't think I'd see you until we got to the church."

"You didn't think I'd let you leave for your honeymoon without training you first, did you?" Elsker shook her head.

"Pardon?" Elsker seemed like such a sweet old lady. I really didn't want her teaching me about honeymoon activities.

"You will be fine, I am sure of it. But you'll be a full goddess in just a few hours. Let's go over using your visions before you fly off to wherever it is Ull's taking you."

"Oh, like you don't know, Norn."

"I would never ruin a surprise." She smiled back at me. "Now sit with your back against the headboard and close your eyes."

I did as I was told. "You're really going to teach me how to use my visions? I'm not a goddess yet. Odin still has to do his part. Will I be able to use them correctly?"

"You will be able to use them well enough. It will be easier for you after Odin completes your transformation, but I need you to have a basic understanding today. I would hate for you to have to summon me on your honeymoon."

Her and me both.

"Inga, Olaug," Elsker waved her hands. "You'll have to clear out. I need space."

"Call us when you're done. We'll be in the kitchen," Inga said as their footsteps padded down the hallway.

"Okay. Keep your eyes closed. Now go to a quiet place in your head," Elsker instructed.

"Shouldn't I write this down? What if I don't remember it?" My hand twitched, wanting a pencil and paper.

"No. No notes. Your subconscious will recall everything it needs to know." Elsker sounded so calm.

"My subconscious has a lot going on at the moment."

"I am ignoring that. Now, picture something anchoring you to the earth, traveling all the way to its center."

I imagined a metal beam shooting from my tailbone into the ground. "Like this?"

"Kristia, dear. You're going to have to focus a bit better than that. Your spirit is turning cartwheels," Elsker tutted.

"Oh. Sorry."

"Picture something *bigger* anchoring you to the earth. A tree trunk, perhaps."

I imagined an enormous redwood with thick, lush bark enveloping me and rooting me to the bed. Its roots stretched all the way to the center of the earth. "Okay. Like this?"

"Well done, Kristia," Elsker praised. "Now I want you to call all of your energy into your body and be fully in the present moment. Are you there?"

"Yes." I took a deep breath and centered myself.

"Very good. Now do you feel the life force surrounding you like a balloon? That is your aura. I want you to put a protection around your aura—it can be anything you need it to be, a plastic casing, a suit of spiked armor, raging elements, whatever suits you.

I visualized a fierce wind whipping in a hundred small cyclones just outside my bubble. There had been a handful of tsunamis off the coast of Nehalem when I was younger, and the biggest one had come during an intense rain storm. The winds had been frighteningly strong, and created a funnel cloud over the ocean. It was terrifying. "Done."

"*Veldig bra*. Now, there are two main ways Norns get information about the future. We use clairvoyance to see images and collect information from those images. Or we visit the tenth realm."

"Ull started to explain that," I admitted. "But he said it was too dangerous for me."

"You're halfway to becoming a goddess now, so you can handle it. Keep your eyes closed, and I will explain." I felt Elsker shift her weight on the bed. "The tenth realm is an alternate reality. It is a harmless enough place, but since all the realms have access to it, it has enormous potential for danger. When you go there, stay anchored to your spirit's cord. If you lose the cord your spirit might get lost between the worlds."

"That sounds scary."

"Just don't lose the cord." Elsker instructed.

Fair enough.

"We're going to visit the tenth realm together."

"Okay." My head still throbbed from Idunn's procedure, but the idea of actually visiting another realm was too thrilling to pass up. I focused on compartmentalizing my discomfort, and tossed the pain box into a far corner in my brain.

"Ground yourself, Kristia."

"Oops. Sorry."

"Now, set your protection on your aura. And imagine a portion of your spirit leaving your body through your belly. At the same time, imagine a cord stretching out of your body. Do you see it?" she asked.

"I do."

"And do you see me?"

My eyes still firmly closed, I glanced to my left. Elsker floated alongside me inside a buttery yellow bubble, led by a silvery string. "I do! What color is my bubble?"

"Can't you see it?"

I squinted at the air in front of me and chuckled. "Sky blue—same as Ull's eyes."

"Naturally." Elsker laughed.

"Okay. Where are we?"

"This is the tenth realm. It looks like Ull's house, but we are actually on a different plane. If you were fulfilling your prophecy we would be searching for our enemies. But seeing as it's your wedding day, we're just going to have a look around the flat."

"Ooh, can we spook Inga?" I asked.

"No. This is an educational trip." Elsker wagged her finger at me. "Besides, she wouldn't see us. She is in the physical realm."

"Oh." There was so much I had to learn.

"Follow me down the hallway. We'll go to the end of the hall and head back to our bodies. It's a short journey, but you have a big day ahead of you."

"Wait—we come to this plane to get information, right? The same way we'd get information from a vision?" I wanted to be clear.

"That is correct."

"So what are we taking from this journey? I know you didn't drag me out of my body just to take me down the hallway." If so, this field trip was even duller than the annual class trip to the lumber farm.

"Oh, sweet girl. You know me too well."

"What is it?" I bounced on the balls of my feet and my aura glowed a brighter blue.

"It's this." Elsker opened the top drawer of Ull's dresser and pulled out a small satchel. "Open it."

She handed me the satchel and I pulled the satiny string. I tipped its contents into my hand and stared. "This is the coin from the British Museum. The one I was looking at the day I met Ull."

"It is." Elsker smiled.

"He took it?" I nestled the coin in my palm and squeezed it.

"He did."

I felt a surge of energy transfer from the coin through my hand—it was like the coin was talking to me. I couldn't help myself; I broke out in a grin that stretched from ear to ear. "He fell in love with me before he ever knew me. He chose me the minute he saw me in that museum, and he's going to spend the rest of his existence doing everything he can to make me feel cherished. I give him the purpose he's been looking for all his life."

"And you know this because?" Elsker prodded.

"I can feel it in the coin." I stared at her with wide eyes. "How is that even possible?"

"This realm exists to convey knowledge. And now that you know . . ." She took the coin and placed it back in Ull's drawer with a smile. "Let's get you to the church. It is time to marry the god I chose for you."

"Oh, Elsker." I beamed at her, my aura sparkling like it was covered in a million tiny diamonds. "Thank you for sending him to me. I'm going to take such great care of him."

"I know you are, sweet girl. Now keep hold of your

cord as you return to your body. Enter through your midsection, and come back to the present."

I did as I was told, and when I opened my eyes I felt lighter than I ever had. My body was absolutely buzzing with energy, and I saw the room with a clarity I hadn't before.

"Well done." Elsker patted my hand from her seat on the bed. "Olaug, Inga," she called. "We are ready for you now."

They came back into the room, each holding a beverage. Olaug handed a steaming mug to Elsker and Inga handed a travel cup to me.

"Earl Grey to-go for the bride." Inga helped me to my feet. "Come on. Let's get you ready to meet your man." She nodded at Olaug and Elsker. "Ladies, we'll meet you at the church?"

"I cannot wait." Olaug smiled at me and I grinned back. I was as ready as I'd ever be.

It was time.

❄❄❄❄

When Inga and I returned to my flat, Ardis, Victoria, and Emma were doing their hair and makeup.

"There you are! Did you get the fit right on your wedding gown?" Emma scurried to the door to take the garment bag out of my hands. She'd bought my little fib. They all had.

"Yep. Just needed a little taking in at the waist." I patted my flat stomach. It might not have been a total lie—I'd probably lost a pound or two between the stress of graduation and visiting my immortal in-laws. And the impromptu brain surgery. Good thing I'd had it tailored just a smidge on the tight side. It would fit perfectly today.

"You know I could have darted it for you." Victoria crossed her arms.

"Aw, I know, V. But I didn't want you working today. You've done enough."

"Well," Victoria conceded. "As long as I get to zip you into your going-away dress."

"Of course. Who else would I trust with that?" I asked. Her wink let me know all was forgiven.

With Inga and me back, we brought the headcount in our little flat to five. There was a bustle of excitement as we jostled for styling space. Emma was distraught to discover her Hair Helper had mysteriously broken. When I caught Victoria's eye she just raised an eyebrow and mouthed, "You're welcome." Well bless her sweet little heart.

Without the strange device, Emma handed over her hairstyling duties. We played rock music and danced while we primped. Ardis swept the top of my hair into a dramatic bouffant and arranged the curls down my back. She gave me a smile.

"It's your wedding day."

"I know." I clasped her hand. This felt like a dream. "I'm glad you're here."

"I wouldn't have missed it for the world." She looked at the ceiling to pull herself together. Ardis didn't let herself get emotional. "I'll be right back—I need another bobby pin to secure the hold."

When she stepped out, Inga came in carrying three boxes.

"What are these?"

She handed me the first.

"It's your something borrowed," she said quietly so the girls wouldn't hear, and I opened the box to reveal an exquisite silver crown. Its peaks formed snowflakes, and etched inside was runic writing.

"What does it say?" I whispered.

"A Norse wedding blessing. It's the sacred wedding crown used by the brides of Asgard. Sif brought it so you could share the family tradition." I was deeply moved and quickly dabbed at my eyes so I wouldn't ruin Victoria's hard work on my makeup. Inga placed the crown on my head, catching Emma and Victoria's attention. As they fussed over its beauty, Ardis returned with a hand full of bobby pins. She gave the crown its due appreciation.

"Sweet." She nodded in approval, composed once again. She pinned the crown in place, and fluffed my hair around my shoulders. I squeezed her hand as she stepped back.

"And what about this one?" I pointed to the second box.

"Your something blue. From Elsker."

"Who's Elsker?" Ardis asked.

Inga didn't bat an eye. "My grandma."

I lifted the lid and found a gorgeous sapphire brooch.

"She thought you could pin it under your skirt like this." Inga lifted my hem. "It's for luck."

"I love it." I had to smile. Dangling from the brooch was the symbol of Freyr, the Norse fertility god. I caught Inga's eye—she was fighting laughter too.

The next box was a gift from Ull.

"Ooh, Kristia!" Emma squealed. The box was small, and I opened it gingerly. We let out a collective gasp. Laying on the softest of fabrics was a small diamond snowflake on a silvery chain. It matched the earrings Ull had given me for Christmas—the ones his dad had given his mom. I touched my ears where they sat, wondering if the necklace was an heirloom, too.

"Wow, it's beautiful." Ardis touched the necklace carefully. Inga helped fasten the clasp and the snowflake sat, looking perfectly at home beside my grandmother's Mjölnir. Inga had been right—Odin had never asked for it back. He'd said it was his wedding gift to me. Well, that and the other thing he was about to do—make me a goddess. I wiped my palms on my sweatpants.

Victoria ducked out of the room, returning with the veil that had belonged to my grandmother. She hung it next to the long garment bag containing the gown Mormor wore to marry my grandfather fifty-five years ago.

"Open it," I whispered. She slowly pulled on the zipper and took out the gown. It looked exactly the way it had in pictures.

"Oh, Kristia." Ardis stood next to me. "She would have been so happy to know you were wearing it."

"I wish she were here," I said quietly.

"She is. In her way."

Ardis was right. I knew a part of Mormor was with us as we looked at her dress. The satiny gown rested underneath a diaphanous lace overlay. Its needlework formed delicate roses and swirling vines, stretching from the fitted bodice down the flowing A-line of the skirt. The jacket of the overlay had long sleeves that ended just below the wrists, and a neckline that formed a much deeper *V* than I'd have expected my grandmother to wear. Pearl buttons ran from top to bottom in the back, and the train was short yet elegant. For a fifty-five-year-old wedding gown, it was seriously sexy.

And seriously stunning. It emitted equal parts elegance and strength, qualities Mormor espoused daily, and qualities I hoped to embody as a wife. The gown appeared to float from its hanger like a soft mist, billowing out in waves at the hemline. With the layers of crinoline under satin and white lace, it reminded me of snowflakes; of clouds; of hope. Of Ull.

It was absolutely perfect.

I stepped into the gown with a shaky breath, thinking about the amazing woman who had worn this dress before me. Had she known the path this gown would take? It was a silly thought, but it was my grandmother who had told me the stories of the North, from whom I'd first heard the then-fantastical names of Odin, Sif, and Thor. My soon-to-be in-laws. It was my grandmother who had worn the silver hammer I always wore around my neck, which I now knew was an Asgardian treasure. I was sure Mormor was in heaven, wherever *that* realm was, smiling at what this day would bring.

When Ardis fastened the veil at the base of my

crown and Inga applied a final coat of gloss to my lips, Victoria gave me her critical once-over. "Perfect," she declared after a moment of interminable scrutiny. It must have been true—Victoria never gave false compliments. "Now go and see how beautiful you are."

My legs barely supported me on my walk to the full-length mirror in the hall. I didn't recognize the girl looking back at me. My cheeks were rosy; my eyes glowed. My hair fell in waves from the half-up-do Ardis had crafted. I squinted at my dress through dewy eyes. It looked so elegant. It was simple, and timeless, and just so, so pretty.

I couldn't believe I was a bride.

Our little group was clustered behind me. Only Inga truly understood the significance of this day, and I was so grateful she was here. I wished I could tell Ardis everything, but secrecy was just one of the sacrifices I would have to make as a protector of Asgard. I hugged them both to me, Ardis and Inga, my past and my future, and we began the short walk to the chapel where my destiny would begin.

When we stepped outside a bagpiper was waiting for us. He started to play.

"Inga." I turned to her with suspicion. She'd gotten a little more involved in the wedding planning than Ull or I had meant for her to. It seemed the day would hold a few over-the-top surprises courtesy of my detail-driven friend.

"You said I could help," she defended herself.

"I said we wanted to keep it simple," I countered.

"What's more simple than one teensy bagpiper?

Besides, this is Wales. They won't let you get married here without one." I supposed she had a point.

Enthusiastic butterflies flounced in my belly. Emma and Victoria flanked my side, and together we made our way the few short blocks to the Norse Church.

When we reached the steps of the chapel, bells rang, signifying that it was time. I leaned over to hug Victoria, but she held me at arms length and gingerly squeezed my shoulders. My eyebrow shot up.

"Ardis said she'd kill us if we messed up your wedding-hair." Victoria shrugged.

I laughed. "That sounds right."

Emma and Inga administered their shoulder squeezes next. "I'll tell Olaug you're ready," Inga said as she led my flatmates into the church. Ardis lingered behind, a smile tugging at her lips.

"You go girl." Ardis leaned in for a gentle hug before she turned for the chapel. "Conquer married life for both of us. Just don't forget me on the other side." She hurried toward the entrance, but not before I saw the moisture in her eyes.

"I could never. You've been my rock all my life," I called after her.

"I think your new rock will take over just fine." She gave a little wave before disappearing from sight.

I fingered the lace wrists of my gown as I stood just outside the door. There was nothing left to do but wait.

Olaug stepped out of the chapel, so beautiful in a pale blue bunad. She led me a few feet away from the door and straightened my train, then she kissed my cheeks and handed me a bouquet of ivory roses wrapped in lace.

"They're from Ýdalir," she said. "I picked them early this morning."

"They're perfect." I inhaled their sweet scent. "Thank you, Olaug, this is so thoughtful." I looked at her closely. "Are you feeling all right?"

"Better than you. I didn't have my brain probed by Idunn."

"You know what I mean." In the drama of the morning I'd forgotten to ask her about my chat with the elf. "You're not really sick, are you?"

"Oh for goodness sake, I am just fine." Olaug shook her head. "Why would you ask Ull to call in the middle of the night? Even wrinkly goddesses need their beauty sleep."

"I'm sorry, really. I was just so worried about you. You are my family, too, now, you know."

"I know, my dear. And you are mine. But gods cannot fall ill. We went over this."

"I remember." I sighed. "That elf guy is really convincing. I was scared for you."

"Well, you need not be. I promise you, I am the picture of health. And I always will be, so long as Idunn provides her apples and so long as my darling granddaughter-to-be does not have her messenger wake me in the middle of the night." She took my hand gently.

"Thank you." I squeezed her back with a smile.

"Are you ready, Kristia?"

"Yes," I answered unhesitatingly. I was ready to be united forever with Ull Myhr. The rest I would take as it came.

Olaug smiled happily. "I always hoped this day would come. My boy does not have to be alone anymore." She patted my cheek fondly, and I felt a lump rising in my throat. She loved Ull so much.

"I'll take good care of him, Olaug."

"I know you will. Come. It is time." She led me to the door and tilted her head. I nodded, and she kissed my cheek before she walked inside to take her seat.

I clutched my bouquet and waited for the music.

CHAPTER FOURTEEN

I ENTERED THE CHURCH alone, ignoring the elaborate garlands strung from the pews—Inga clearly hadn't stopped at the bagpiper—and the people who turned to stare at me. The only thing my eyes saw at the end of the short aisle was Ull, exquisite in his black bunad. Pewter buttons at the calves held red tassels, and he wore an intricate red vest topped with a coat made so beautifully it had to have been crafted by Olaug. His normally disheveled hair was styled with uncharacteristic neatness atop his head, and his brilliant white teeth peeked out from upturned lips. But it was his eyes that captivated me, drawing me forward although my legs felt too weak to walk. So pristine in clarity, bluer than any clear sky, they were crinkled from his joyful smile. I wanted to run to his side.

When I finally reached the front of the church, Ull held out his hand. As I lay my palm on his, the enthusiastic butterflies fell still. Ull's touch sent warmth through my body, filling me with a calm I hadn't felt all day. It pulsed through me, the absolute knowledge that this was where I was meant to be. There was no question everything we'd been through had been worth it. Fending off Elf Man; standing up to Thor; learning about Ragnarok; falling in love, despite Odin's rules; fighting for this love, even when the universe was stacked dead against us . . . every moment of heartache had been worth it. Because now I stood at an altar with the god I knew I'd love from now until the ends of all the worlds. And I was about to become his wife.

I looked at my love, my own eyes echoing his happiness, and squeezed his hand in anticipation. In a matter of minutes, Ull would be my husband. We'd be bound together, our souls entwined for as long as both should live. Which, considering the whole immortal thing, was a very, very long time. And I wasn't just tying myself to Ull—I was getting Olaug, Inga, Gunnar, Sif and Thor, too. I was minutes away from being a part of a real family.

It was what I'd wanted my entire life.

"You look beautiful, Kristia." Ull leaned down to whisper in my ear. "That dress is just . . . wow."

I beamed up at him and touched the tear at the corner of his eye. "I love you so much."

"I love you, too," he whispered back.

Odin stood before us, enormous in stature, made all the more impressive by his exquisite golden robes. I would have been intimidated if I wasn't so focused on Ull's chiseled cheekbones; the masculine line of his jaw; the feel of his skin on my hands as we prepared to pledge our lives to one another. It was overwhelming, in the best possible way.

"Marriage is an age-old contract. Once merely a legal means to an end, today it signifies so much more. Years ago, people did not marry for love. They married for strength—to strengthen family lines through the procreation of children; to strengthen providences through the alliance of families; to strengthen spirits, gaining someone to live for. The notion of a romantic love was once as foreign as I am sure my dress appears to some of you." Odin gestured to his robes and the congregation chuckled. I snuck a look at my flatmates as they nodded. Victoria probably had heaps to say about a man dressed in a shapeless gown.

"And for a long time, I thought the notion of a romantic love would prove too foreign for my grandson. I thought the notion of *any* love was more than he could process. He is as stubborn as he is intense, and for a number of years I had resigned myself to watching him live out his days alone.

"But then you came along." Odin's gaze shifted to me. "You, the most foreign thing to us all, opened his eyes to a future he could not see. You opened his heart to a dream he abandoned long ago. And you opened his spirit in a way none of us dared hope for.

"In marrying Ull, you give him a life he might have imagined, but never once expected. And in doing so, you give me the greatest blessing I could ask for: my grandson's happiness. I am, eternally, in your debt."

Odin reached for my hand and pressed it gently against his lips. "Thank you, Kristia," he whispered, before straightening his back and adjusting his sleeves. From the heat on my face, my blush must have crept all the way to the roots of my hair. But Ull just gave me his rakish half-smile, looking at me with eyes the color of a cloudless sky, and making me feel like we were the only two people in the room. My embarrassment faded with the squeeze of his hand, and I steadied myself as Odin asked us to repeat after him.

"I, Kristia, take thee, Ull, for my lawfully wedded husband." My voice cracked over the last word. *Husband*. I drew a shaky breath and pushed forward. If I stopped to think about how overwhelmingly happy I was, I'd never make it through the rest of the ceremony. "To have and to hold, from this day forward. For better. For worse." The lump in my throat rose. "For richer. For poorer." My eyes filled with moisture. "In sickness and in health. As long as we both shall live."

Ull reached up to cradle my face. He wiped my tears with the pad of his thumb, then leaned in to plant a kiss on my forehead.

"That part comes later," Odin chastised, much to our guests' amusement.

"*Jeg elsker deg*," Ull whispered as he pulled away.

"I love you too," I whispered back.

Ull pulled his shoulders back and repeated Odin's words. They wrapped around me like a warm cocoon, enveloping me in the security of their pledge. "I, Ull, take thee, Kristia, for my lawfully wedded wife. To have and to hold, from this day forward. For better.

For worse. For richer. For poorer. In sickness and in health." His eyes misted over as he spoke the final line. "As long as we both shall live."

My eyes spilled over at the sight of Ull's solitary tear, and for one endless moment we stood, Ull stroking my face and me staring at the deity who had pledged his life to mine. As impossible as this day had seemed, every moment within it felt absolutely right. Ull had been my destiny all along.

As Odin said the words that bound us together, Ull's eyes bored straight into my soul. Joy radiated from every part of his massive being. I'd never seen him like this, and I desperately wanted it to stick; happiness suited him.

Odin folded his hands and his voice dropped. "Please face me," he commanded. A lump burrowed in my throat. Ull raised a questioning eyebrow and I gave a slight nod. I was as ready as I would ever be, but after this morning's "procedure" I was also a smidge terrified. If this part of my transformation felt anything like the other part, our friends were in for one heck of a show.

Odin picked up an enormous hammer and began to sing. Mjölnir was magnificent in person. It was easily the size of a smallish dog or largish cat, depending on your allegiances, and it shone with a brilliance that more than hinted at its divine origin. Odin's voice rang through the chapel, voicing the magic that would change me forever from Kristia Tostenson, mortal, to Mrs. Ull Myhr, Goddess of Winter and Protector of Asgard. Ull squeezed my fingers and I let out the breath I hadn't realized I was holding. *Breathe, Kristia. It can't possibly be worse than this morning. Just breathe.* I waited, but the pain never came. Instead, I felt my brain getting warmer. The build became more intense, but it didn't hurt. It felt like I was filling with energy, the cells of my chest buzzing frantically and bouncing off one another. The warmth created a deep peace that radiated slowly, traveling down my spine to my back, and then to my arms and legs before reaching my tingling extremities.

As the warmth came back to my head I felt so light, so full of joy and brightness, I was certain it must be noticeable. I glanced at my friends but they seemed unaware of my transformation. Only the Norse party bore recognition, their heads bowed in reverence.

Another jolt surged through my spine, drawing my shoulders back and elongating my torso. The energy traveled upward, tiny bubbles of energy popping along each vertebra until my head felt like it was filled with my favorite pink champagne. As each bubble popped, it filled my brain with a memory that wasn't my own. I saw the creation of the worlds, born of the darkness that stretched between fiery Muspelheim to icy Nifheim. The disparate climates mixed together, lava merging with the glacial river until realms filled the darkness. I saw the birth of the races from the jotun, Ymir; the creation of the cow Audhumla, whose appetite freed the ancestors of Odin. I saw Odin fashion the earth from Ymir's remains, and craft mortals from the trees he found by the sea. I saw Odin's marriage to Frigga, the birth of the Æsir, and their daily meetings at the world tree, Yggdrasil.

Then my visions changed, zooming in on each scene as its bubble rose into my head. I saw Idunn creating the magical apples. Then my frame of reference tunneled through the apple to its core, so I could see the immortality formula on a molecular level. I saw Tyr, the God of War, as he led Asgard's army into battle against the residents of Muspelheim. Then I saw him administer the fatal blow to a trio of fire giants. Bloody streaks obscured my vision as his broadsword pierced the boil-ridden flesh of his victim.

I saw a woman I knew was Freya leading a herd of flying horses, each bearing a beautiful female warrior on its back. I zeroed in on one as she dove over a human battlefield, easily wresting a fallen soldier in her arms before taking off for Odin's hall at Valhalla. I saw the battles of a millennium—attacks by frost giants, ogres, trolls and dark elves, all in the amount of time it took Odin to finish singing his verse. As his voice reverberated on his ending note, I saw one final vision. A little blond boy climbed the back of a couch to stare out a window. Outside, Sif gave a small wave before taking Thor's hand and walking out of sight. She wore her sword in her belt, and carried a backpack that must have contained battle provisions. The little boy pressed his palm against the glass, warm breath fogging the cold surface. His shoulders sagged and his little body started to shake. Olaug came up from behind, pulling him firmly into her lap. She held the boy while he cried, murmuring something in his ear I couldn't make out. When he looked up, she brushed his tears away with her wrinkled fingers. Then she took his hand and led him to the kitchen, helping him onto a stool and handing him a carton of eggs. His face lit up as he attacked his task. His little tongue stuck out of the corner of his mouth, and when he finished cracking the last egg he looked at Olaug with such a proud expression, my heart tugged. She beamed back at him, kissing his forehead and dusting his nose with one floured finger. He laughed as he started to measure out the sugar, his tears now forgotten.

I blinked and the vision disappeared. But my glimpse into Asgard's history—and Ull's—was something I wouldn't soon forget. Nor would I take it for granted. Ull's world . . . my world . . . balanced on the back of a thousand battles. Our freedom depended entirely on the ability of its warriors to defend the realm. And to fight those battles, our warriors *and their families* had to make sacrifices of their own. It didn't escape my notice for one moment that the security of Asgard had required that little boy to say goodbye to his mother without knowing when she might return. It broke my heart.

But my husband would never need to feel alone again. Now that I was truly his equal, I would spend every moment of the rest of my existence showing Ull exactly how much he deserved to feel loved . . . and giving him the security of family he'd never been able to count on.

I would do absolutely anything for that god.

My body was filled with energy when I looked up

at Ull. His jubilant smile mirrored my feeling that all was right in my world. His steady hand was firm on mine, the only thing that kept me from floating into the rafters of the chapel. We turned back to Odin, who repeated the last line of his song in clear verse. With that, we heard the words that made us one.

"I now pronounce you husband and wife. Ull, you may kiss your bride."

My eyes met Ull's in an elated dance. We'd done it! He swept me in his arms, his hands pressing my back tightly against him. I could feel the thud of his erratic heartbeat as his breath hitched. I reached up to touch his cheek, marveling at the wedding ring nestled perfectly on my left hand. Ull raised an eyebrow. He angled his head down and stared at me in a way that set the brigade of butterflies free in my belly. His eyes said *get over here*.

And they were inky blue.

Ull pulled me into his chest and kissed me so soundly I forgot the people around us. Forgot the sanctity of this holy ground. Forgot that my new in-laws were watching. The only thought in my mind was this man—my husband—kissing me, claiming me, and loving me absolutely beyond reason. It was the best feeling I'd ever had, and I wanted to hold onto it forever.

❄ ❄ ❄ ❄

"Come, my love." Ull pulled me toward the side door of the church. The ceremony was over and our guests had retreated to the hall for cocktails and hors d'oeuvres. We'd just signed our marriage certificate and it was time to join the party.

"Where are we going?"

"You shall see." He tugged at my hand and opened the door. A blast of cold air hit me in the face. Ull took off his coat and wrapped it around my shoulders as he led me to the courtyard. The roses and ivy were swathed in twinkle lights, and hurricane glasses held ivory pillar candles that shimmered in the twilight.

As I stared, I realized I could hear the gentle flicker of the lit candles. The soft popping of the burning wick hummed lightly in my ears.

Whoa. That was new.

I exhaled slowly as I looked around the courtyard. "What is all of this?"

"I thought I could put Inga's exuberance to good use. I asked her to recreate Ýdalir for us."

"That's really sweet. But why?"

"So I could give you a romantic dance under the stars at our wedding." He'd remembered.

"Ull." My cheeks felt warm. This was too much.

"Mrs. Myhr." He held out a hand. "May I have this dance?"

"Of course." My voice was barely more than a whisper. Ull put his hand on my waist and gently guided me around the courtyard. I rested my head on his chest as we moved slowly in the square, not caring for once whether I tripped over my own feet. I knew Ull would catch me if I fell.

"Thank you, Kristia," he murmured.

"For what?"

"For choosing me. For agreeing to take on

everything that comes with being my wife. For giving up your own life to be a part of mine." He pulled back to look at me. "For letting me see that I do not have to be alone anymore."

I stretched my neck as high as I could, still a foot from his face even in heels. He met me halfway, bending to kiss me fiercely. I knew people were wondering where we were. I knew it was rude to keep our guests waiting. But I easily could have stood in that freezing courtyard kissing my brand-spankin'-new husband for the rest of the evening.

Ull pulled back to examine me closely.

"What?" I was suddenly self-conscious.

"I am just wondering how you feel. Did it hurt? You were so composed."

"You mean when Odin changed me?" He didn't know what Idunn had done this morning, and I wasn't about to tell him now. I took a mental inventory. "I feel fine."

"Are you certain?"

"Well I do feel a little warm, or I did when we were inside anyway. And kind of tingly, like all of my nerves are bouncing off each other. Like those awful computer diagrams of the atom from junior high science class, you know?" He probably didn't know. The school in Asgard had bigger fish to fry than teaching its teenagers about the particle.

"And I'm a little lightheaded. But that's probably not related to my changing." I reached up to twirl a lock of his hair.

"So you really feel all right?"

"I feel much better than all right." I stretched up to kiss him again. When I pulled back he was beaming.

"I thought I was meant to live alone. And today . . . I have more than I ever could have imagined."

"You're stuck with me now," I teased. "No take-backs."

"No take-backs," he agreed solemnly. He fingered my curls. "Your hair." He smiled. "It is glowing."

"What?" I grabbed a strand in alarm. That couldn't be good. How was I supposed to be incognito with glowing hair?

Ull laughed. "It is not actually glowing. But look at it."

Staring at the strands around his finger I could see what he meant. My normally dark-blonde hair had a sort of luminescence to it. It wasn't lit up like I'd feared, but it was definitely different. Almost like the midday sun was catching it and reflecting back a golden hue much brighter than my natural color, though the only lights out here were candle and twinkle.

Ull unwrapped the strand from his finger and held it up. "It is beautiful."

"Come on." I grabbed his hand, not wanting to be distracted by any other changes I hadn't yet discovered. "Our guests are waiting."

"Let them wait," he growled, and twirled me around the courtyard. I was amazed that I stayed upright—he really was a good leader. Or was it possible that now that I was immortal, I really was less clumsy? I'd hoped for as much during my little procedure. *Oh please, please.* It would be so fantastic if I not only got the world's most perfect husband today, but I also got just a teensy bit of grace. Just a little bit—I didn't need to be greedy.

"Now this night only needs one more thing to make it perfect." Ull curled his fingers into a fist. He opened his hand, and a small cloud hovered just above his palm.

"What the . . ."

He blew lightly on his palm and the cloud floated overhead. It grew as it moved, until half the courtyard was covered with a billowy white foam. Ull tapped his finger against the air and the cloud let loose with a light flurry of perfectly-formed snowflakes that dusted the cobblestones in a light layer of white. My head swiveled up, and I closed my eyes as the flakes brushed my cheeks. When I opened them, Ull looked down at me with a soft smile.

"I thought it was time I showed you what we can do."

"We?" It took me a moment to register the words. I was too busy staring at my own personal Norse god framed by his homemade flurry. "You mean I can do that too?"

"I am not sure. You will be able to do it, yes. Whether you are able to control it at this moment, I do not know. Would you like to try?"

"Lord, yes." My fingers twitched. I didn't *feel* any differently, but I definitely wanted to give it a go. "What do I do?"

"Focus on the quadrant of your brain where you

most felt the transformation. Was there a particular spot that felt it the strongest when Odin triggered the change?"

No. But there sure as Sherlock was a spot Idunn had made particularly sore. I assumed Ull was referring to that place.

"What do I tell that spot to do?" I avoided the question.

"Channel the weather pattern you wish to effect, and draw it to your fingertips."

I pictured Ull's snowstorm and visualized it traveling from the still-tender spot in my brain down my neck, through my arm and to my hands. My fingertips immediately felt chilled.

"Whoa."

"Exactly. Now bring them into a fist, starting with your pinky, and open your hand."

I did as I was told. But instead of a fluffy white cloud hovering obediently, a sharp icicle shot from my palm like a bolt of lightning. It wrapped itself around a tiny critter scampering up the tree, freezing it in place.

"Oh my God I killed a squirrel!" My hands fell to my side as my jaw fell open. I threw my head into Ull's chest and moaned. "I am the worst goddess ever."

Ull's throaty chuckle made me look up.

"It's not funny. I. Killed. A. Squirrel."

"He is not dead, Kristia. Watch." Ull pointed a finger and an orange stream floated toward the animal. It thawed the frost, and the squirrel continued his ascent up the tree as if nothing had happened.

"You can make heat too?"

"Of course. We need to be able to make corrections as needed. Sometimes we will not get a weather pattern right on the first try. This is Odin's way of making sure we can control the elements—*all* the elements." Ull touched the side of my neck. I could still feel the heat on his fingertips.

"That's amazing." I shivered. "But I'm not doing it again until we're somewhere no woodland critters can be harmed. I can't have squirrel blood on my conscience."

"Fair enough." Ull smiled. "We can practice on our honeymoon. No squirrels where we are going."

"Is that a clue? Somewhere with no squirrels . . . are we going to a desert?"

"Guess all you want, Mrs. Myhr. I will never tell. But I will dance." Ull pulled me close and began to move. My head settled comfortably against him as he led me in a small circle beneath the twinkling lights.

I didn't know how long we'd been outside before I heard the impatient click of heels on the courtyard. We were swaying slowly, my cheek pressed firmly against Ull's chest, when Inga cleared her throat.

"Are you two planning to come to your own party?"

Ull laughed.

"We were enjoying your creation." He gestured with one hand to the lights, the other wrapped firmly around my waist.

"I see you added your own touch." Inga stared at the cloud, still emitting gentle puffs of snow.

"Just to show Kristia what she can look forward to.

Everything you set up was perfect."

"Yes, yes. I'm a visionary. Well if you don't come inside soon, Thor is going to eat all of your wedding cake. And there's a lot of cake." She tapped her foot.

"Inga, we said simple!"

"Four tiers *is* simple. What? I could have gone for seven like I saw in last month's *Modern Country Wedding* magazine. That one required a special infrastructure. At least your cake stands on its own. Mostly."

"What do you say, my love?" Ull looked at me. "Are you ready to join the party?"

"Well . . ." I gave him a wink. "I do like cake."

CHAPTER FIFTEEN

OUR RECEPTION WAS A wonderful blending of our friends and family. We had traditional Norwegian and contemporary American food. The Asgardians particularly liked the mini-sliders; the small burgers disappeared as Thor guiltily licked his lips. My roommates loved the Norwegian waffles we served after our meal, and everyone enjoyed the enormous chocolate cake we cut, playfully smearing the icing. When it was time to end the celebration, my friends and I ducked into the small bride's room at the end of the church. Ardis and Inga helped me change out of my grandmother's gown and into the sassy, ivory going-away dress Victoria had designed. It was a sleeveless lace number that hugged my curves and ended three inches above my knees. This dress had a higher neckline than my wedding gown, but dipped in a low *V* in the back. And its lace formed a bolder pattern, with beads generously embroidered throughout the needlework. As I stepped into the sky-high heels Victoria had chosen, I reached reflexively for something to hold before I realized I could balance on my own. Victoria zipped me into the dress and fastened the pearl clasp as she gave me one last hug.

"I need to borrow the bride for a minute." Elsker pulled me into the hallway, leaving my girlfriends giggling in the bride's room. "Are you ready for this?"

"I hope you're not asking about what I think you're asking about, because I got your wedding gift and I have to say—"

"Oh, that." Elsker waved her hand. "Yes, Olaug and I want great-grandbabies."

"Elsker!"

"I meant your new life, silly. Are you ready for everything to change?"

"Do I have a choice?" I was about to leave on my honeymoon. I really didn't want to think about the whole *Seer* thing right now.

"No. And things are going to change big time. You'll see things more clearly: past, present, and future. We will have a lot of training to squeeze in when you get home from your trip, but now that you are an Asgardian, you are eligible to fulfill your prophecy."

My prophecy was hardly the first thing on my mind as Ull strode down the hall. I locked eyes with my new husband. He ran his eyes up and down the contours of my *very* fitted dress as he approached, and winked. My stomach flipped.

"Kristia. Pay attention." Elsker swatted at me.

"Sorry."

"Now that your powers are realized, you must be

more careful than ever. Every enemy of Asgard will be after your gift. Do not leave Ull's side while you are away."

"Do not worry." Ull slid up beside me and wrapped his arm around me. "I will keep her next to me the entire time."

My cheeks got hot. Why did he have to look at me like that in front of Elsker?

"And her new security detail will be waiting when we get home." Oh, great. The bodyguard. Well, at least I got to enjoy my honeymoon in peace.

"If you see anything unusual, anything at all, call me through your necklace. I will find you immediately." Elsker hugged me fiercely.

"Thank you, Elsker. For everything." I hugged her back.

Ull kissed Elsker on the cheek. "Come, Kristia. It is time." He poked his head into the small room. "Goodbye, ladies."

My friends rushed to the door and wrapped us in a group hug.

"Have a wonderful trip," Emma bubbled.

"Have *fun*," Victoria teased.

Inga cuffed Ull on the shoulder. "I expect you to be significantly less grumpy when you get home."

Ull laughed. "Shove off, Inga."

"You two trying to sneak off without saying goodbye?" Gunnar's voice came from the end of the hallway. When he reached us, he slapped Ull on the back. "You kids behave yourselves while you're away." He waggled his eyebrows suggestively. "Or don't."

Ull's grin stretched from ear to ear.

"Seriously, mate. Take care of our girl." Gunnar kissed my cheek, then pulled Inga to his side. "Kristia's family now. We have to look out for each other."

At his words, Ardis threw her arms around me. When she pulled back, her eyes were moist.

"Oh, Ardis!" I pulled her to me again.

"I just love you so much," she blubbered in an uncharacteristic display of emotion.

"I love you too." We held each other tight. After a minute, Ull gently rubbed her shoulder.

"Come visit us soon, *ja*?"

"Try and keep me away," she sniffed. She gave me a wink. "Go. Honeymoon. Tell me *all* about it when you get home. I want every. Last. Detail."

Ull glanced down at me. "Shall we?"

"Absolutely." I placed my hand in Ull's and he led our little group through the church, and out to the garden where Ull had first opened up to me. My heart filled with happiness. We walked hand in hand the short distance to Ull's car as our friends tossed English rose petals. Inga must have arranged for someone to hand them out. Their fragrance filled the air, sweet and light.

Ull closed my door before walking to his side. He started the car, and rolled down the windows to hear the well wishes of those we loved most. We waved through the back window and drove off into the night.

Ull took the narrow paths out of Cardiff, reaching the expressway in no time. He held my hand as he easily maneuvered through the traffic with a relaxed smile on his face. I kept sneaking glances at his perfection when I thought he was focused on driving. I'd catch him beaming every time I did. How was it possible this incredible creature was now my husband?

We reached the private airstrip much quicker than I'd thought possible. Ull drove through the gate and parked next to a small jet marked NORSK1. He shrugged when I raised an eyebrow. "Guess I forgot to mention this too, eh? One of the perks of Asgard, for when we need to travel like humans." He got out of the Range Rover, stretching his long legs as he walked around to open my door.

"How much haven't you told me?" It seemed impossible that there could still be more surprises.

Ull tossed the keys to the waiting valet while easily wresting our luggage from the trunk with one hand. "Kristia, darling, we have eons to discuss trivial details like family jets. You know the important things—none more important than the absolute commitment of my love for you." He leaned his tall frame down to kiss my neck just below my ear, the most effective spot for ending my conversation.

We boarded the plane to the welcome of the most beautiful flight crew I'd ever seen. Ull seemed unimpressed, but I couldn't help but stare at the stunning flight attendant, her silken, chocolaty hair flowing to her waist, holding flutes of a sparkling beverage on a silver tray. She was tall and willowy—the picture of absolute physical perfection.

"Welcome Mr. Myhr. Mrs. Myhr." She smiled,

revealing perfectly white teeth beneath ruby-red lips. "Congratulations on your wedding. Would you care for a beverage?"

"Thank you, Stacey." Ull grinned at her. "How was your flight here?"

"Uneventful, sir."

Ull raised one eyebrow. "Was it really?"

"Well . . ." Stacey grinned back. ". . . there might have been a few undesirable elements on our exit from Asgard. But nothing we couldn't handle." She handed Ull a bubbling flute, then turned her smile to me. "Mrs. Myhr? Champagne?"

"Um, yes. Please." I took the glass. "Thank you."

"Gunnar told me about the battalion of fire giants you ladies took out last week. Well done."

"It was nothing," Stacey demurred.

"That is not what I heard. Gunnar said you were trapped in a cave with an injured horse and still managed to take out seven targets with a broken broadsword. Impressive." Ull nodded.

"Well, those fire giants always were slow." Stacey blushed at the compliment. "Now, if there is anything you need before your flight, just let me know. I will be up front, preparing your appetizers."

"Thank you." Ull raised his glass. I watched as the woman sauntered to the front of the plane, moving with a grace that rivaled Inga's.

"What is she?" I murmured. There was no way she was a human.

"A Valkyrie," Ull whispered conspiratorially. "Our battle goddesses." He led me to the center of the cabin and placed my bag under one of the couches.

"And they're in charge of your airplane? I thought Valkyries flew winged horses?" I tried to remember my grandmother's stories.

"They will drive anything that flies. They are not particular. Best pilots we have." Ull shrugged, unconcerned. "Shall we begin our honeymoon, Mrs. Myhr?" He nodded to the oversized chair and I settled comfortably into its cushions. He sat beside me and I curled up against him. It had been an exhausting day.

"How do you feel now?" Ull asked once we were safely in the air.

"Happy." I ducked my head so my hair hid my sudden bout of shyness. "I can't believe I'm your wife."

"I am the one who is in disbelief. You have taken on so much by marrying me. I cannot fathom that you would do that for me." He looked at me closely. "Do you feel . . . different?"

"No visions since the wedding, if that's what you mean. Is that bad?"

"No, darling. Believe me, nothing would make me happier than you being vision-free. You will continue to keep me in the loop when things affect you?"

I bit back a smile. It didn't matter one bit that I was a goddess now; Ull would *always* fret over me. It was sweet as strawberry pie.

"I cannot help but worry about what you plan to do. But I trust you will let me know if you feel overwhelmed with any of this." He grazed the tips of his fingers along the inside of my elbow, and I nearly dropped my glass. Just then, the world's prettiest flight attendant came to top off our champagne.

"I'm not overwhelmed, Ull. I promise." I turned to Stacey and smiled. "Thank you. This is delicious."

"Of course. Your appetizers will be ready in just a moment." She retreated to the front of the cabin and Ull kissed my forehead.

"You look absolutely incredible in that dress, my love." He traced a finger along the *V* of the neckline and gave me a look that seemed to shoot sparks from his eyes. In that instant they shifted from icy azure to inky midnight. I shivered.

God, I loved that color.

Ull pressed a button on his seat and the lights in the cabin dimmed. A loud click came from the front of the plane, making me jump. "What was that?"

"I just turned on the *do not disturb* sign."

"But Stacey just left to make appetizers. And we've barely taken off. Why would you—"

I was cut short by a god nibbling on my earlobe.

"Do I need to spell it out for you?" he murmured.

My mouth formed a small *O*. No. No he did not.

Ull scooped me onto his lap. "Get over here, wife."

Spirited butterflies wreaked havoc in my belly. Ull continued his ministrations to my ear, twirling a complicated pattern with his tongue in the sensitive spot just behind the lobe. I shuddered as a wave of contentment rocketed through me. A slow burn worked its way across my skin, my pulse keeping time with the rhythm of Ull's mouth. As he worked his way down my neck, I drew shallow breaths in a pointless effort to control my pounding heart. My pulse quickened, growing more intense with each movement of Ull's lips. He made his way toward my collarbone, raking his teeth over the skin. And then . . .

Oh my God. My eyes rolled back in my head as Ull shifted me on his lap. His hands locked tightly around my waist as he began tracing the neckline of my dress with his tongue. It was hot against my skin, which suddenly felt like it might burst into a thousand tiny flames, if not from the proximity of the Norse deity doing insanely amazing things, then from the anticipation of what was *finally* going to come next.

"Ull." The word came on a breath. I shifted my weight, driving the hem of my skirt up another inch. Ull pulled his hand off my hip faster than a goose could fly off a griddle. Before I could bemoan the loss of contact, I felt his palm on my bare knee. The touch sent smoldering embers up the length of my leg. My eyelids flew open—inky-blue eyes stared me down. One corner of Ull's mouth turned up as he rested his forehead against mine. And then he inched his palm upward, spreading his fingers so he gripped my upper thigh.

It was the first time he'd touched me like that.

"This okay?" His thumb rubbed a slow circle on my leg, sending my already-heightened nerves into apoplectic hysteria. The butterflies beat a frenetic rhythm in my abdomen, which clenched in a way that sent my head spinning. He'd touched my leg—*just touched my leg*—and I was ready to black out. How on earth was I going to make it through what I desperately hoped was coming next?

"This okay?" Ull repeated. I managed a small nod before Ull dropped his head. He ran his nose along the line where my skin met the dress's lacy strap. Then he pressed his lips against the material. The heat of his mouth seared through the thin fabric of the gown, and I twisted in his arms. Ull stilled, then he threw me over his shoulder and carried me to the back of the plane.

"What are you doing?" I giggled.

"What do you think?" Ull kicked open the door to a small room. It was barely large enough for the bed, entertainment unit, and wet bar it held, but somehow I didn't think space would be an issue. Ull deposited me onto the bed. Without turning around he locked the door behind him, and lowered himself so he hovered me. He kept his weight on his forearms, but I could still feel the weight of a six-foot, five-inch idol resting against me. It was intense. Exhilarating.

And something I wanted to experience privately. *Not* within earshot of a ridiculously hot flight crew.

"Ull!" I squirmed. "We can't do this here!"

"Why not?" He ran his nose along my shoulder. "You are my wife; the love of my existence. You look stunning in that dress. And I have been waiting literally forever to be with you. Why delay?"

Well, when he put it like that . . .

"Because." I struggled for words as Ull lifted one arm over my head. His lips brushed the insides of my wrists and my head spun. "Um . . ."

"Exactly." Ull kissed his way down my arm, drawing a figure eight pattern with his tongue when he reached the inside of my elbows.

"No. Hold on." I forced myself to think. "I can't do this with witnesses. It would be too embarrassing."

"The crew would never come back here." Ull drew his fingertips down my ribcage, pausing at my hip. As he grazed my thigh, I put a hand to his chest.

"Trust me, I want this. Way more than you do. I've practically been begging you for this for months. But when we do this, I don't want to worry about other people being around. When do we land?"

"Three hours." Ull kissed my arm.

"Ull?" I lifted his chin with two fingers and forced him to meet my eyes. He let out a sigh heavy with frustration.

"What is another three hours going to kill?" He rolled off me and stared at the ceiling.

"Precisely." I pressed his palm to my lips and nestled my head in the crook of his shoulder. "Besides, we wouldn't want those appetizers to go to waste."

"I have no problem wasting the appetizers," Ull growled.

"I know."

Ull stood and crossed to a mini-bar in the corner of the bedroom. He returned with two champagne-filled flutes.

"To an extraordinary honeymoon, Kristia Myhr."

My heart soared at the sound of my new name. So much had changed in the last year. I'd gone from the timid loner in the one-light town to an international co-ed. I'd experienced a physical transformation that all but killed me, and joined the gods in an immortal existence. And I'd married a guy who was more myth than man, whose very existence defied everything I'd ever believed to be true. Nothing in my life was even close to what it had been twelve months before. I should have been freaking out—leaping from the airplane screaming like the proverbial banshee.

But the truth was, I'd never felt more like myself. After nineteen years, I had direction. It would take me a while to get there, but for the first time in forever I could see why my path had been so convoluted. And I could see exactly where I was meant to go.

The best part was knowing that Ull would be with me every step of the way.

"To our honeymoon." I clinked my glass against Ull's. Honeymoon with my Norse god. I was definitely in over my head.

I wouldn't have wanted it any other way.

OLAUG'S NORSK WAFFLE RECIPE

3 eggs
¾ cups sugar
1 dash baking powder
1 tablespoon vanilla sugar
¼ tablespoon cardamom
½ cup melted butter
1 quart of milk
Flour to taste (approximately 5–7 cups)

Whip eggs thoroughly, then mix in sugar. Add baking powder, vanilla sugar, and cardamom together, and blend. Pour in butter and milk. Add flour until mixture reaches desired consistency. Yields one pitcher of waffle batter.

Serve with a tart jam. Or Nutella . . .

STAY TUNED FOR A
SNEAK PEEK OF…

THE ELSKER SAGA:
TRO

ACKNOWLEDGMENTS

To the amazing man who champions all my crazy dreams—thank you for making me your family. To our beautiful boys, who bring hope, light and so very much joy everywhere they go—we're so grateful God gave us you.

Mange takk to the supportive writing-friends, who held my hand along the way. A million thank-yous to the truly incomparable Stacey Nash—I can't even begin to express my gratitude for everything you do for me, so I'll just promise the next time Inga goes out of town, Gunnar is all yours. Shh!

Thank you to my 'technical advisor' Nicki, who opened my eyes to the Tenth Realm. Heaps of gratitude to Eden Plantz, for always keeping Kristia strong. And many thanks to Lauren McKellar, for pushing our gods to new heights.

Tusen takk to the readers who continue to champion this little story. I'm truly humbled by your support. RagnaRockstars, y'all rock in every conceivable way. Thank you for keeping me laughing.

And to Olaug, whose warmth and strength inspired a saga. *Takk* for everything. Always.

ABOUT THE AUTHOR

Before finding domestic bliss in suburbia, S.T. Bende lived in Manhattan Beach (became overly fond of Peet's Coffee) and Europe...where she became overly fond of McVitie's cookies. Her love of Scandinavian culture and a very patient Norwegian teacher inspired her YA Fantasy series. She hopes her characters make you smile, and she dreams of skiing on Jotunheim and Hoth.

Find S.T. on her website at www.stbende.com, or subscribe to her newsletter at http://smarturl.it/BendeNewsletter .

WANT MORE OF THE NORSE CREWS?

Meet the God of Winter and his Norse crew in
THE ELSKER SAGA.
THE ELSKER SAGA: TUR (a novella)
THE ELSKER SAGA: ELSKER
THE ELSKER SAGA: ENDRE
THE ELSKER SAGA: TRO
THE ELSKER SAGA: COMPLETE BOXED SET

Meet the God of War and his Norse crew in
THE ÆRE SAGA.
THE ÆRE SAGA: PERFEKT ORDER
THE ÆRE SAGA: PERFEKT CONTROL
THE ÆRE SAGA: PERFEKT BALANCE

See the crews together in the bonus Elsker/Ære
crossover novella . . .
SUPERNATURAL CHRONICLES: THE ASGARDIANS

And meet the demigods in
NIGHT WAR SAGA.
NIGHT WAR SAGA: PROTECTOR
NIGHT WAR SAGA: DEFENDER
NIGHT WAR SAGA: REDEEMER

See what happens when the goddess next door honeymoons with the Norse God of Winter in...

THE ELSKER SAGA: TRO

Sometimes you just have to believe.

Finding her destiny nearly cost her everything. Kristia knows she can handle whatever The Fates throw at her next--including her long-awaited honeymoon with the God of Winter. But as things heat up between Kristia and Ull, a frost settles over Asgard. An unexpected death marks the beginning of the end, much earlier than anyone expected. Kristia's barely begun to understand what she's capable of, and controlling her powers seems completely out of her grasp. With her new family fighting for their lives, and Ull fighting for their future, Kristia has to make a devastating choice: preserve the life she loves, or protect the god she can't live without?

Here's a sneak peek at the next chapter in Ull and Kristia's story...

THE ELSKER SAGA: TRO
CHAPTER ONE

"Down you fall, into a sleep;
Monsters all, with you, shall creep.
Demons joyful, spirits fly,
For the gods, at last, shall die.
Goodnight little ones."

THE SHROUDED FIGURE FINISHED *the disturbing lullaby on a sharp note, her scratchy voice reverberating through the otherwise quiet nursery. She clutched three bundles as she stood. Her silhouette easily stood twenty feet in height; she made an imposing figure against the arched window. She crossed the room with awkward strides to deposit each bundle in a crib. With the babies safely distributed, she moved to the rocking chair and touched one gnarled finger to a piece of paper. Her eyes were hooded, but even in semi-darkness, I could see the joy behind them. Her mouth curved into a menacing smile, yellow teeth poking at sharp angles against purple lips.*

"Sleep well, my little darlings," she croaked. "Your prophecy is a thing of beauty. The Fates expect great things of you." She dropped the paper onto the chair and walked out of the room, directing an eerie smile at each crib as she left. Then she closed the door tightly behind her.

I crept toward the note on silent feet, careful not to

disturb anything more than the air. It was a cavernous room with forty-foot ceilings, and heavy tapestries that lined the walls. Three cribs sat beneath an imposing chandelier. The three bundles slept peacefully, their hushed breathing the room's only sound. But the bundles weren't making the kinds of cooing sleep sounds I'd expect of newborns.

Now they were stirring, the movement loosening the bindings on their swaddles. Their faces were still obscured in shadow, but I was struck by the unnerving realization that these babies were nothing like human babies. One let out a guttural hiss; the other a soft growl. And the third made a noise so animalistic, it sounded like a wail . . . or a war cry.

As the cacophony in the nursery reached a fevered pitch, I darted for the rocking chair. Without thinking I grabbed the note and stuffed it in my pocket, then I made a dash for the door. Whatever those babies were, I didn't want to be around them any longer.

My hand burned as I turned the knob. I jumped back, cradling my fingers. The skin pulled across my bone; large blisters had already begun to form. Someone, or something, had turned the metal molten. Maybe it was a defensive spell, something to protect the children. With any luck, I'd never know. I pushed through the pain and gripped the doorknob again, wrenching it open and bolting down the hallway. I ignored the searing ache in my palms as I pumped my arms, willing myself to reach the exit faster.

Heavy footsteps thudded behind me. They were slow but determined, each step closing the distance between its maker and me. I didn't have to turn around to know an angry giantess was bearing down, and I didn't want to think about what she'd do if she caught up.

Ducking my head, I tore around a corner and bolted for the doorway. It was close, only ten yards away. When I was halfway there, two heavily armed guards stepped into my path. They were easily thirty-feet tall, each with an array of weapons attached to a thick belt. One held a spear in his hand, while the other wielded a broad sword. Both locked me in their sights and charged. My head whipped back and forth—the angry mother closed in on me from behind. The guards were fast approaching from ahead. My only option was to hide.

I turned on my heel and bolted through the closest doorway. Now I was in some kind of recreation room with large chairs, a blazing fireplace, and, thankfully, high windows flanked by thick curtains. My legs burned as I dove behind one, curling into a ball and willing my breath to come in quiet gasps. It might have bought me a minute, tops, but a minute was all I would need.

Thundering footsteps announced the giants' entry. They crossed the room with angry shouts. The language was foreign but the sentiment translated easily enough. A few more seconds, and I would be deader than a doornail.

My blistered palm wrapped around my grandmother's necklace as I squeezed my eyes shut. I drew on my happiest memory of my sinfully gorgeous husband, Ull. Just that morning he'd stood at the altar of the little church in Cardiff. He'd been the most beautiful creature I'd ever laid eyes on, watching me walk up the aisle with near-worshipful eyes. The smile playing in his lips and the gratitude in his gaze were images I'd remember for the rest of my existence—no matter how short it might be. The footsteps stopped just beyond my reach, and I knew the guards had found me. It was only a matter of time before they ripped down the curtains and eliminated the threat.

Hopefully, it would be over quickly. Pain had always been my undoing.

The silver replica of Thor's hammer began to warm in my hand, and I opened my eyes. Beams of light radiated from between my fingers in bright flashes. They were sure to give away my location, but I didn't care. I knew exactly what was happening.

It was taking me home.

I squeezed my necklace as the guards tore down the curtains. The beams increased in intensity, striking the guards in the chest and throwing them back. The angry giantess stormed across the room, hands outstretched and ready to strike. Before she could reach me, I was sucked into the air, my insides churning under the unbearable pressure as I hurtled through darkness. My bones felt like they might rip clear out of my body, and the pounding in my head was so insistent I danced precariously along the edge of consciousness. Just before I could pass out, I remembered the note. I tore it from my pocket as I hurtled through space, determined to see its contents before I woke up from this bizarre vision. The paper shook in my hands as I strained to make out the words. This prophecy would spell the fate of the three babies. It would explain why their giantess mother was overjoyed at its news; and why my very presence had driven her to a rage. Whatever it was, whatever their fates, my gut told me the prophecy and those children had deep ties to my new family.

I unfolded the note. Hastily scrawled letters told the future of the three newborns from the nursery. The prophecy marked a new beginning that necessitated a violent end. It contained only two words.

End Asgard.

I closed my eyes as the bile rose thick in my throat. And then I was consumed by darkness.

❄❄❄❄

"Sweetheart. Wake up." The voice in my ear was soft yet commanding; the words managed to be both a plea and an order. My eyelids fluttered, and I buried my face against the warmth beside me. It smelled of earth, and pine.

It smelled like home.

"Wake up *now*, Kristia." The warmth moved away from my cheek, and when I dragged my eyes open I found myself cradled in strong arms. The magnificent blond deity looking down at me had a furrowed brow, set jaw, and the perma-stubble that was so characteristically Ull. Even on his wedding day, he couldn't bring himself to shave.

"Hi," I murmured as I rubbed the sleep from my lids. All thoughts of my nightmare were instantly forgotten as I lost myself in my brand-spankin'-new husband's endless blue eyes.

"Hi yourself." Ull brushed a lock of hair off my face

and lifted me so I was positioned tightly against him. "Must have been some dream."

"Hmm?" I dragged myself away from the whirlpool that was Ull's gaze, and absorbed my surroundings. Opulent couches equipped with seatbelts, a small table holding half-empty champagne flutes, and an entertainment unit that would rival my fantasy of a Hollywood screening room. Asgard's private jet was equal parts elegance and comfort, and right now it was barreling toward the mysterious destination where Ull and I would spend the first night of our married life.

Oh, God. Our wedding night. I swallowed hard as I tried not to over-think that one.

"Are you cold?" Ull reached behind him to pull a blanket over my bare legs. The skirt of my going-away dress had inched up another few centimeters, so it barely covered the tops of my thighs. Now the expanse of exposed flesh was being massaged by Ull's rather sizeable palm.

I flushed. "Not anymore."

"Good." Ull leaned down to press his cheek to my forehead. "Now, are you going to tell me why you were yelling in your sleep? Did you have another vision?"

I struggled to remember the images that must have troubled my dreams. But for the first time, something had slipped through the normally firm grip of my subconscious. Flashes of colors came to mind—dark purples, menacing crimson; and feelings—desolation, fear, and . . . joy? That made no sense. Those feelings went together as well as peanut butter and pickles.

"I don't know what I was dreaming about." I shook my head. "I can't remember it."

Ull's brow furrowed against mine. "Is this common? Have you forgotten your dreams before?"

"Not that I can think of. Usually they're right there when I wake up." I shrugged. "Must not have been important, I guess."

"You were screaming." Ull spoke softly. "You sounded afraid."

"Really?" I squeezed my eyes shut and tried to force the dream back into my consciousness. But it was gone, filtered from my memories like water through a fishing-net. "Sorry. I have nothing."

I opened my eyes and blinked at Ull. He was frowning at me.

"I do not have to stress to you the importance of your visions. If they—"

"I know." My fingers grazed his arm.

"You are the Seer—and now that you are immortal, this makes you Asgard's strongest defense. If whatever you envisioned is something that might come to fruition, it is imperative that you share it with me."

"Sorry, Ull. I've really got nothing." I shook my head. "You know I'd tell you if I could."

"If you think of anything, *anything*—"

"I know." I raised a finger to stroke the stubble along his jaw. "I'll tell you right away. You know you don't have to worry about me all the time."

"Kristia you are my world. Of course I worry."

I sighed. Ull was innately protective—his position as an Asgardian warrior gave him every right to expect the worst could happen to the people he loved. But ever since our favorite Norn, Elsker, had declared I was this long-prophesied visionary the gods dubbed the Seer, he'd taken protective to a whole new level. Because I was privy to visions of the past, present, and future, I was the shiniest new weapon in Asgard's arsenal. I was also one of our enemies' most highly sought-after targets. And with everything we'd just been through, my six-foot, five-inch, immortal assassin was terrified that somebody would take me away from him.

It was kind of adorable.

"Is there any chance we could just enjoy our honeymoon?" I moved my finger along Ull's jaw, over his Adam's apple, and down the hollow of his neck. My palm rested against his chest; the thud of his heart beat a steady rhythm against my skin. "Please?"

"That look is not going to work on me every time, you know." Ull sounded frustrated.

"Then why is the corner of your mouth twitching?"

"Because. That look *is* going to work on me ninety nine percent of the time, and you know it." Ull chuckled. "All right. I will drop it. But only because we are here."

"We are?" I leaned across Ull's lap and tried to raise the window shade.

"Not yet. Trust me, you want to see the whole picture. Not just a sliver of it." He tightened his arms around my shoulders as the plane touched down. In seconds it came to a stop, and the world's loveliest flight attendant walked out of the cockpit. She pressed a button on the side of the plane and a door opened, inviting beams of sunlight into the dim cabin. It was a shock after spending several hours in semi-darkness, and I blinked against the brightness.

"Sorry sweetheart." Ull reached into my bag, then placed a pair of sunglasses atop my nose. He cupped my cheek in one hand. "I forget how sensitive your eyes must be."

It was true. Enhanced vision was just one of the side effects of becoming a goddess. But if the sparks shooting off my cheek were any indication, my sensitivity to Ull's touch was going to be much more problematic.

"Come." Ull stood, stretching his long legs and holding out a hand. I placed my fingers in his and followed him to the front of the plane, tugging at the hem of my dress as I moved. "Leave it," Ull ordered without looking back. "I like it up there."

The temperature in my cheeks tripled.

"Mr. and Mrs. Myhr." Our flight attendant tossed her chocolaty-brown hair over one shoulder. "Welcome to Asgard Cay."

"Thank you, Stacey." Ull nodded as he stepped out of the plane. He reached into his pocket and pulled out a pair of aviator shades. He put them on, and turned to me, hand outstretched. "Are you ready?"

There was no way I could ever be ready for this—my first day as an immortal, starting my honeymoon with a Norse god. So I did the only thing I could. I closed my eyes, took a breath, and put my hand in his. Then I stepped out of the cabin.

"Let's do this."